THE DUKE IN HIS CASTLE

Vera Nazarian

Copyright © 2008 by Vera Nazarian
All Rights Reserved.

Cover Paintings:
"Portrait of a Gentleman in his Study" c.1527, "Christ Taking Leave of his Mother (detail)" 1521 by Lorenzo Lotto.

Interior Illustration: "The Duke" by Vera Nazarian, © 2008

Cover Design Copyright © 2008 by Vera Nazarian
(with Erzebet YellowBoy)

ISBN-13: 978-1-934648-43-8
ISBN-10: 1-934648-43-4

Trade Paperback

June 15, 2008

A Publication of
Norilana Books
P. O. Box 2188
Winnetka, CA 91396
www.norilana.com

Printed in the United States of America

THE DUKE
IN HIS
CASTLE

Norilana Books
Fantasy

www.norilana.com

Other Books by Vera Nazarian

Dreams of the Compass Rose
Lords of Rainbow
Salt of the Air
The Clock King and the Queen of the Hourglass
Mayhem at Grant-Williams High (YA)

In Memory of My Father

For Wendi who read it first
For Stella who shared her home
For Giles who gave advice
For Erzebet who loved it

The Duke In His Castle

A Novella

Vera Nazarian

ক্ষ I ঞ্জ
Starting On A Lighter Note

The Duke stands outside in the courtyard of his castle. In his mind he is at the bottom of a well, within a funnel of wind and air. He is withstanding an onslaught, buffeted by a formless *influence*—neither a being nor disembodied reflex—a pressure of something that has the texture of infinite crystalline facets. No breeze touches his skin, yet the tiny blond hairs along his arms covered with shirtsleeves are raised, bristling at the invisible something, or nothing, bristling in futility.

The Duke is young and pleasing in a primeval way; he evokes an instinctive attraction. He is replete with proportional flow of line and surface, one giving way to the other in a perpetual continuation, with smooth plateaus of skin covering a delicate facial bone structure, with curving wisps of gilded wheat hair combed back in a queue, or sometimes lying loose and wanton about his shoulders. Wanton is not something of which he is aware and yet it is a property of his self, together with smooth and silken and virile and decadent.

The castle is scattered in crumbling pieces of relic and ruin on all sides of him. Massive faded walls of grey and mauve and violet moss-covered rock, grand fissures straining from the onslaught of creeping vines and insidious grasses, fractal chaos of skyline amid meager patches of open sky—they all press down on him, fill his lungs with sepulchral stagnation and slow his heartbeat to the rhythm of clockwork, ever winding down. Each breath the Duke takes is slower than the last, it seems, each one carries death a moment closer, yet never quite enough. His youth stands as a buffer between the gaping maw. Youth? He would tear it out of himself with all his fierce will, to have this existence end in the next blink.

Only, he cannot.

Confined within the bounds of his castle, Rossian, the Duke of Violet, softly wanes.

ଔ**ନ୍ଧ୍ନ**ଧ

"**M**y Lord," says the elderly liveried butler in measured tones, "The man is at the doors again. With the . . . remains. Should I let him in?" The butler wears a starched, impeccable coat of deep plum velvet, near-black, as ancient as the bedrock of the castle, with shirt and cravat of fine threadbare linen washed ten thousand times into a consistency of cobwebs, and cufflinks of antique gold. Beyond the gnarled fingers, his fingernails are buffed and manicured; his mustache trimmed, and the ashen hair gathered in an orderly queue. Not a speck of lint, not a hair out of place. Always deliberate responses; composed and placid, swamp-colored eyes.

The Duke ponders this interruption while standing near the window. The room he inhabits most often like a native shade, his favorite room, is claustrophobic, with walls of immeasurable thickness closing in on him, crude ancient boulders of granite concealed by dust-drenched tapestries and hangings upon which pastoral and courtly scenes are enacted, populated with stylized figures representing nobility, kings and queens and emperors and hierophants, and occasionally a beast hunted in the woodland thicket.

There are other such rooms in the castle, and he samples them over the years. Though, it seems there are always that many more left unexplored, untouched; chambers are endless pristine spaces in a honeycomb, containing whatever ancient dross or treasures the mind can only surmise at, and often as such they go unrecognized. A glimpse in one of them might reveal volumes from the lost library of Alexandria underneath a thick sheeting of dust, or a handful of Atlantean coins found at the bottom of a distant sea and brought here by galleon, their surface luster disguised by encrustation of barnacle and salt. The possibilities skim across the mind, ghostly leftovers of human curiosity, which the Duke finds less and less in himself. . . .

The moment of dazed abstraction passes and the Duke turns his gaze away from the beckoning daylight, while in back of his mind trying to ignore the pressure of a thousand pounds of stone. "The man?" he says quietly. "What?"

"Sir. Need I repeat the description? The same one, remotely mercantile in some distasteful manner or another. Definitely vulgar. The one who claims to have the bones and dust of—ahem—Nairis, the Fabled One, and who also claims that Your Grace is the only one who can restore her to life."

A startled flicker comes to the young man's eyes. They are violet-blue places of murk, and now they are agitated. "Life, life . . . bringing to life. Bones and dust . . . Nairis, the Fabled One . . ." he mutters, listening to the sound of words as they drift in the chamber. Then, emerging from the daze, "What, not this nonsense again? Didn't you tell him once to be gone, and that I'm busy? Remind him, do, that despite my considerable abilities and learning I know of no power in the world—no ritual sorcery, no psychic magic, no blood-letting sacrifice, not even charlatan smoke and mirrors—that can return the dead to this mortal coil with true permanence."

The butler clears his throat, swallows phlegm; a chronic habit. "Absolutely, my Lord, I told him, speaking as plainly as possible. But the man is obviously a raving buffoon. He does not appear to believe me. And now, I'm afraid to say, he threatens you with some mischief."

"Hah!" the Duke snorts, beginning to pace the room, its floor of creaking ancient wooden timbers. The butler watches a shelf of flimsy bone china bric-a-brac perched precariously near, figurines trembling with each step. The Duke is indifferent to these dubious heirlooms of pasty Dresden pink and gilded white, and yet here they sit—have sat thus for years, dancing in porcelain palsy at his frequent outbursts.

The Duke raves. Words flow in a stream now; he is unstoppable, and he uses language high and low, an interwoven entity fleshed out of anger, ragged barking elements that echo in the chamber, pound in dull torpor against the fabric insulating the walls and ring in clean violence against the exposed stone of the lofty ceiling.

"What has the world become? Why, the world's a pock-marked backside of an ass! Or is it the front of an ass? Nay, a breeding place of dribble-spit idiots and lunatics, insolent upstart commoners daring to threaten blue bloods!"

"Another thing, my Lord. There is also a young . . . female creature at the doors. Very oddly attired, scandalously, I must add. And with no attendant menservants. She claims to be sent by the Duchess of White."

"Hell and Damnation and Pestilence and Pox! Not in the mood for that again, not at all. No more vile cousins-fifty-seats-removed and their minions snooping around, looking for the essence of my *secret*—their secret, everyone's secret!—all uselessly. And staying for a fortnight or two, eating out my pantries and emptying my cellars—woe to my ancient wines, my cognac!—not that I care a whit for that filthy piss-sour cognac, blast it to smithereens, but still, they never even offer thanks for it. Instead, endless tedium, broken only by the agony of a myriad questions posed by asses. Jackass braying is what I get, bray, bray, bray. Punctuated by idiotic, meaningless prods into my nature which have nothing to do with anything but succeed in ruining meals."

"I remember, my Lord. The Duke of Blue's minion inquired once after the color of the spot at the base of our smallest billygoat's rear left hoof. Something to do with the mark of the devil on livestock. And we don't even have goats."

The younger man gives him a sharp look.

"My Lord . . . It is my business to recall such things. In any case, what should I do about your callers?"

The Duke visualizes pouring rain, a deep gully filled with pea-soup mud and his callers dunked in it, all in one tangled mass of limbs and plastered clothing and human tedium.

"I suppose you must let the wench in," he says, savoring the word "wench" as though it were a chunk of fresh crusty bread and he sinks his teeth into it. "No use having the White Duchess disgusted by our rudeness—just yet (we'll be sure to disgust her in excess, later). But the vendor—mischief indeed!—tell him to get out of my castle and off my lands and never to come back if he wants to keep his nose and his precious ancient remains intact!"

The Duke pauses. "No, wait, that's too trivial. Nose, precious remains, no. Tell him that he should not return here unless he is prepared to lose a limb of his body and a decanter of blood. I shall ravage him with my teeth."

"Yes, m'Lord, as you say." The butler inclines his head just in time to conceal a little smile of satisfaction, and exits.

When the thick door shuts behind him, Rossian allows his features to go slack. Longing emerges once again, dredged out of some abysmal repository of raw and half-formed instincts inside. His eyes lose focus, gaze returns to the rectangle of daylight, and he slowly nears the window, its ledge carved into a flat crude fissured shelf of rock, a place to lean with the elbows.

Once more he strives far ahead, and his thoughts are winged and lustful, crimson and orange-feathered birds; they circle out there in dust-mote specks, where the brilliant sky rises over the gaily colorful countryside with its bucolic fields and meadows, mushroom colonies of tiny thatched roof cottages in the distance, and a curling strip of mirror-brightness where the river winks in and out of being along the horizon. The land, as far as the eye can see, as far as a lustful bird-thought can fly, is all his.

Yet Rossian, Lord over this domain, has never been outside the grounds of his castle. It is simply that he may not; he *cannot*.

The young Duke is virile and hale. He is in full possession of mobility in all his limbs, and he carries inside him a steady heart which (despite the vertigo illusion of slowing clockwork) continues to serve him well. And yet, the Duke never looks up and down the full breadth of sky without its edges framed by crumbling walls. He never takes more than a dozen steps in direct sunlight, never lacks shelter from drenching rain or soaks up fully-formed banks of mist with his skin.

Only his spirit wanders forth. And his imagination.

Now, Rossian shivers and looks away, as though coming awake, but as always it is only from one level of dream into another. He inhales dust; he sees disarray, the careless arrangement of the room, the infernal tapestries with dynasties of dead kings, bookcases of abandoned, long-untouched volumes bound in faded brown vellum (after years of obsessive perusal he knows their contents by heart; they never need be opened again), a shelf of flimsy knickknacks that he despises but which supposedly belong to his departed mother and for that he holds on to them as though they were her ashes.

And now there is the imposition to consider—a half-conscious awareness of immediate reality, a wash of cold existence, a grounding. *Truly*, he thinks, *it is only with the coming of my unwanted guests, that I come to life. Maybe I should be grateful to them for dredging me out of the dreaming swamp.*

For what innumerable time he wonders what a particular relation, in this case, the Duchess of White, is like—for she too is imprisoned and he has never seen her in person and never will. He wonders what kind of pet, acolyte, messenger, spy she sends this time. Of all his noble relations, she is the fifth—maybe sixth—to investigate him thus, leaving only the Dukes of Green and Yellow who haven't yet bothered to pay him a visit through the necessary proxy. It's a veritable circus, this Ducal family circle of theirs. He has seen a half a dozen circuses; knows them well, for they come to the castle to entertain and shock and invoke pity, as they make rounds of the countryside with their wagons and sequins, their caged beasts, grotesque freaks, and acrobatic fire-eating charlatans.

Circus or not, there is no doubt whatsoever: an ancient curse lies upon the Dukes of this realm—this field and meadow

Eden-country sprawling beneath the uncharted infinity of sky. This curse makes his existence what it is, a simmering unending purgatory of suspended being.

Ages upon centuries upon decades and seasons and days ago, the so-called Just King rules all, and they—the Dukes and Barons and the Knights—having amassed great wealth through valor, accomplishments and power, think themselves equal to him and imagine their veins filled with a liquid the color of heaven. They rise in rebellion. They are bright, fierce, arrogant in their blue blood, and the struggle fills codexes of history. When blue blood is spilled, it flows plebeian red, but the ground is hungry for whatever hue as long as it is thick with the residue of life.

Eventually, the Just King, no less a sorcerer than a statesman, quells their revolt. He employs an intricate combination of artifice and force, and is merciful as his name.

The great-great-grandparents of the modern Dukes are not put to death. Instead, a *binding* is laid upon them and their heirs unto eternity. How the King concocts it is unknown to history or speculation. And yet it is an amazing sort of thing; a simple, cruelty-lacking, gentle torment; a death without dying, a spillage of blood without the breaking of skin, anemia without leeches.

The binding amounts to a curious kind of imprisonment—without walls or physical restraint. Neither the Dukes nor their heirs, those children who become Dukes or Duchesses after them, can leave the grounds of their home castles or strongholds. It's as if an invisible wall of resilient air springs all around, and they cannot venture a step outside. Many try, of course; indeed, all do. They use fierce will, passion, anger, physical effort, sorcery and guile, but naught comes of it. Nothing can, for an unconditional binding of such magnitude is designed to contain.

The great grandparent of the Duchess of Orange, it is said, brandishing his ceremonial sword and cursing at the sky, rides his battle steed at full gallop through the open front gates of his castle. It is to the effect of meeting a steel wall. While the stallion races on undaunted, the rider is thrown and falls dead to the ground on the *inside* of his own castle land. Upon examination *medicalis* and dissection, he is found to be crushed to death by the pressures of what amounts to a mound of quarry stones.

Another brave ancestor, the grandmother of the Duke of Black, feeling that her parody of life is not worth a blade of grass, decides to jump out of the window of the highest turret of her castle. It is a suicide, a sin of outrage against the divine, and no matter if she falls to the ground, or dies in some mysterious way such as a volley of heavenly lightning and thunderclaps— nothing is too unexpected—she swears she would be satisfied. She is prepared for flames and eternal damnation. She is not prepared however, simply to step off the window ledge, only to feel the invisible wall support and hold her aloft in the air, and not allow her further movement outside. There she flounders suspended between the heaven and the earth, a human fish caught in the airy ocean net, a cod, a mackerel, a gasping carp with prodding limbs instead of gills. It is then that the neighboring villagers looking up at the castle witness their first miracle.

Other miracles follow. One Duke has his life miraculously saved when he is shot upon from the outside. The enemy projectile bounces off an invisible *something* as soon as it reaches the boundary of the castle grounds; the curse is revealed to hold its own blessing.

I want none of it, none, thinks Rossian. *The only blessing is to end, quietly, maybe while submerged in a bliss-dream. I will never find out all the secrets, and I will not try. What remains then is slow decay.*

The *secrets.* . . .

It is rumored that when the Just King lays his binding all those ages upon centuries ago, he also bestows upon the Dukes a single hope of redemption, of an eventual freedom from the curse. The curse itself is everlasting, but it does not disallow a way out. All have been given, supposedly, a different secret power to be passed on through the heir in their lines. When a single Ducal heir discovers *all* of the secrets of the others, he or she will be free of the binding. . . . And maybe then the sky will fall, and the subterranean well waters will rise and flood the land and torrential heaven waters come down from on-high to fill the rivers past their banks—and once the waters from above and below meet, there will no longer be green meadows and verdant fields to plow, only swampland and mist. . . .

And freedom.

Now, locked up in the strange prisons of their own castles, the great-great grandchildren of the original traitors send endless messengers and spies to one another, in spring or autumn, in winter and summer, some in the guise of a proxy friendship "visit," others not bothering to hide their intent at all.

Each one tries most desperately to discover the secret power of every one of the others. Having no means to accomplish it in person, each has to rely upon the adequacy of trustworthy and guileful messengers, usually other relatives. What a grand heirloom joke the Just King sets in motion all these ages ago! A punishment of endless self-inflicted hell; with in-laws, to boot, in every sense of the word.

"Excuse me? You *are* the Duke of Violet?"

The door to his study has been soundlessly opened while

he is lost in thought.

Rossian winces at the ringing timbre of the speech. His grimace intensifies when his gaze, accustomed to aesthetically soothing blandness and order, locates the actual source of the disturbance.

The female creature—for no one sane would call it "woman"—the creature peeks from the open door, head first, then fills the doorway with the rest of her terrifying self, and enters. On her head she wears a peacock screaming-green page cap. Its foundation of fabric is obscured, for the cap is festooned with layers of natural materials that might be employed by nest-building birds or rodents—branches and ivy and wildflowers, tufts of moss, several small apples threaded and attached with a rainbow of satin ribbons. The ribbon ends are weighed with bells and there are bunches of baby's breath stuck in spots along the brim. If the cap were a Yule table centerpiece, it would be too garish. If it were a bird's nest, it would frighten magpies.

The rest of her outfit clashes with the headgear in a chromatic fury, and in that way manages to complement. Her upper body is assaulted and consumed by a great doublet of various shades of orange, many generations out of fashion and many sizes too large, while lower down there is harlequin's masculine hose. One leg is Sherwood Forest green and the other crimson with black stitching at the seams that dares to mimic a highlands tartan. The hose fits loosely like old skin over thin limbs, and suddenly the gaze is drawn to a ludicrous codpiece stuffed with rags.

Lower yet, hose disappears into a halfway-presentable pair of soft leather boots, of an unfortunate shade of deep plum purple. For accessories, there's a long knife—culinary? —stuck at her wide saffron belt that cinches the voluminous doublet around a waist of indeterminate girth. Finally she is topped off by an enormous oversized charm-locket on a thick silver chain, hanging around the neck down to the approximate level of her stomach.

What makes this creature female? From underneath the cap the Duke sees a little-girl face. She is a whimsical doll; two grand eyes with a manic shifting expression, round fat cheeks, a tiny rosebud mouth. And yet, in the manner of an expensive heirloom doll, she is somehow old.

Indeed, thinks Rossian, the face is the only thing about this creature that does not offend; though, possibly the offense will make itself known in time. All else is revulsion, a festering wound to fine blue-blood sensibilities.

What a grotesque contrast they make. He, a gaunt vertical shadow with expensive refined airs, violet eyes, violet reflections in his wanton hair like dark honey; she, a whimsical squat toy-creature of vulgar insanity.

And what's worse, she is holding a red, black and gold funeral box.

"No . . . " he says, feeling suddenly faint. "Not *that.*"

"Yes," she says in a voice as bright as her outfit. "Here, my Lord, are the dust and bones of Fabled Nairis! Or, is it—that is to say, maybe, possibly—Nairis, the Fabled One!"

"Who the devil let you bring this—this *thing* in here? And who are you?" His tone is harsh, desperate. In his mind, stones and ice are grinding together.

She blinks, and a sudden confused darkness comes to her. The veneer of garish clothing may as well be non-existent, for with that one blink she is funerary while her words have lost their joyful charge and are falling like rain. "Who? Only the butler, my Lord, I think. He allowed—that is, he did not protest sufficiently—that is, I am not implying *I* am the butler, of course, no. Oh! I'm Izelle . . . Lady Izelle, my Lord. First cousin of Her Grace, the Duchess of White."

"*Lady* Izelle. Lady? God-in-chattering-heaven. And what might be the purpose of this visit, pray I ask?" Rossian's voice cuts past the rainfall like a finely honed scythe. He has a wicked talent for it, since childhood; furthermore, there are so many opportunities to practice it.

The lady however seems to catch on immediately. There is a mercurial switch. "My Lord, before I even bother with an explanation, you didn't answer my original question. Are you the Duke Rossian? Or are you his poor relation?"

"Just call me Hanger-on Robbie." In his mind he smirks; he is gearing up.

"Aha, well then. Robbie, is His Grace available for—"

"Oh, for heaven's sake. There is no Robbie. I am the misfortunate you were instructed to seek. And as you can see, my luck has indeed run out, for you have located me. I am at your . . . mercy."

The Duke inclines his head in the faintest semblance of a bow.

The monstrous doll's rosebud mouth curves into a wicked smile.

"Then, Your Grace, I appreciate your mercy if not your service. And thus, let me be straightforward with you, in my haste to alleviate your suffering. I am here for the sole and resolute purpose of finding out your precious secret, so that my Cousin can take her first walk outside. Preferably next moon."

He throws back his head, looks up at the stone ceiling, notes a cobweb garlanding one corner. He laughs softly. "You are a precious sort of jester, do you know? Wherever did she dig you up? First cousin, you say? No, that's impossible. Blue blood is incapable of producing *you*."

The Duke turns to the door to call his butler. "Harmion,

is this some kind of clever joke on your part, to provide me with *nouveau* sublime entertainment on a much too lovely afternoon spent yet again indoors? Why did you not announce her? She let herself in somehow, past your Cerberus guard."

From the hallway comes a familiar phlegmatic cough, followed by a clearing of throat.

"Apologies, my Lord. I was not given the opportunity due to the Lady's rush of movement up the stairs. One would be reminded of a hound pack. And no, m'Lord, never a joke," Harmion says tonelessly on the other side of the door. "I'm afraid this is quite beyond me."

"There, see," Rossian says to the creature. "You are even beyond Harmion. Therefore, you must be a figment of my degenerate, sickly mind. Only I can be depraved enough to imagine you. If I close my eyes, will you depart?"

He gestures with disdain at the funeral box. "As you make yourself gone, please be sure to take it with you. Merely by its nature, whatever is inside, it is repugnant to the living. Not to mention, blasphemous and out of place here. Relics, even fake ones, are meant for chapels and tombs, not drawing rooms. In short, I will not lower myself to ask how you acquired it, but I find its presence in my chamber unacceptable."

Quite as unacceptable as you, he begins to say, but doesn't. Instead he closes his eyes as promised, playing his own game.

When he opens them within moments, she is still there.

Izelle watches the Duke, her doll-face stilled in an attentive calculating expression. She is possibly evaluating his degree of gullibility even now, measuring him up against the others she has had the pleasure of tormenting, in order to report the exact details to her infernal Duchess.

"Do I truly disgust you?" she says suddenly. Indeed, as

she has promised earlier, she is blunt. But the manner in which she appears to savor the notion is odd and fascinating, and the Duke finds himself startled.

"This box of venerable remains is distasteful to you, but what of myself, my Lord? Obviously it is so. And yet, you are a blue blood, so where are your manners? Do you always pay such scathing compliments to your guests? No, really, you can't be this rude."

"I cannot help it, you're a clown, madam," the Duke replies. "For that matter, you're not a guest."

And the creature before him appears to be stunned into momentary silence. It's as if up to that point she has no idea that she is indeed a grotesque, a jester, a terrifying costumed scarecrow. Or maybe she docs. Wait, yes, the Duke sees a smile held back in the rosebud mouth, a smile pressed hard against little dainty teeth, he imagines. . . .

"My Lord," she says softly. "Oh, I like you! You are rude and yet formal as the vestments of a bishop at high mass, a piquant combination! Sarcasm and stuffy decorum and wicked mercy, all in one man! Oh, whatever words shall I use to describe you to my Cousin? I can't imagine. Have you a pictorial likeness I might take back with me, to show Her Grace? A lacquer miniature, perhaps?"

He gapes at her swift change in humor—that she remains standing in this small claustrophobic room before him despite his command to depart, that she is undaunted and is in fact laughing at him.

"I hope there's one thing you come to understand," she says. "That nothing you say will make me leave. Hate me, despise me, be nauseated by me and this pretty bones-trinket, but here we are. We will stay until we learn what we must—this Fabled Nairis and I. Right, my dear?" With a grin she looks down fondly and pats the funeral box (it is the moment at which the Duke first seriously considers that she is indeed insane, and as a secondary thought, wonders what is contained in that box of death).

She, meanwhile, continues, "You may be rude enough to force me physically, to call the butler and a legion of servants—but I can resist. Both you and your men. And your sorcery. It's rather quite unladylike of me, but as you say, I am a clown, and a very determined one. In truth—" and here she gleefully closes her hands and arms about the funeral box in a morbid embrace, "I do believe I'm going to enjoy myself here. When is dinner served?"

She ignores the Duke, ignores his eyes—which are dilated in outrage at being subjected to her insolence. She glances around the study—for this chamber obviously doubles as a personal library and a sitting room—and her gaze takes in minute detail.

He watches her in fascinated horror. His lips part as she suddenly moves toward the nearby writing-table of heavy antique mahogany and plunks down the box beside an open volume of esoteric philosophy, next to sacred yellowed pages that are liable to crumble from a too-strong breeze. . . .

And then she adds insult by speaking yet again. "Duke, my sweet, while you yourself appear to be clean, presentable, and debonair, this room, my Lord, this whole castle of yours, is one big compost pile. Yes, do not flinch now. Decrepitude and rot, everywhere. On the outside, weeds. Within, dust and dirt. Look around you! How can you allow these magnificent things to sit in such filthy conditions? Volumes of Maneille, and the Fire Magus, unshelved and littering a table! Ancient references removed from protective sleeves and left to grow brittle in sunlight! The encyclopedic works of *Alghieri's Sorcery* shelved out of order and in most cases lying spine-down or flat on top of others—really, something must be done about this, immediately!"

"Harmion!" he cries, unable to bear it any longer. "*Out! Get her out!*"

"Oh, come now, tsk-tsk," she says. "I suppose—I surmise you really *don't* understand. If you prefer not to listen to anything else I say, then consider this. Not unlike you, my Lord, Nairis, this poor creature whose deathly remains are here before you, disgusting you so, was an Heiress to a Dukedom. An Heiress to Yellow, I believe, or possibly Chartreuse, as that noble branch calls itself. The man down below in your foyer who was peddling this item, told me all about it, which naturally got me interested enough to take her remains off his hands. And because of what she is, or was—do you follow my logic, Sir?—the curse of our kin applies to her also, even in death. Which means that she—or her remains—once brought in, cannot be normally removed from the confines of this castle. Can't even be budged—I've tried it, and so has the unfortunate vendor. Why else do you think he would not leave?"

The Duke listens to her while things cold and slithering start moving in his mind, slow gears of a gigantic rusted machine.

"Now, unless you would like this box to grace your entryway permanently," Izelle continues, "you might consider cooperation. I venture that only with my Cousin's sorcerous help might you remove this annoyance. Indeed, I can almost promise it—Cousin knows many things you'll never guess. But—only after you agree to cooperate with me, or at least deport yourself civilly toward me. Now you see why I brought her—that is, Nairis—in here. Lucky coincidence? Thank heavens for traveling merchants who threaten mischief."

Rossian's jaw rises and he wets his lips. "But—what nonsense," he says. "Are you *blackmailing* me with that thing? Do you think I really care whether an idiotic relic—no matter how distasteful to me—is somewhere in my castle? If it can't be taken outside, I'll have it removed to some far corner and stowed in a cellar. Anywhere out of my sight. And it wouldn't bother me."

"Oh, but obviously it *would*, my Lord; to quote the Poet, *thou doth protest too much.* Any fool, even a jester such as myself, can see that you're afraid of it for some reason. What is it, the stench of death? Or the implications?"

"Damnation and nonsense yet again. Why should I be afraid?"

"I don't know. Not yet. And really, it simply doesn't matter for now. However, I promise you, at some point I will find out."

The Duke looks at her, anger suspended behind a mask of stone. "If it doesn't matter, then why in the world are we talking about it? I still don't understand what the devil kind of leverage *she,* this deceased Nairis, represents for you against me—in your mind, verily, only in your mind! Devious, nasty little thing, are you? Your White Duchess certainly picked a gadfly to send as my tormentor. Only, regardless of your ability to sting, whatever either of you expects to find here, is . . . not."

He pauses, breath failing his voice. He feels emptiness, a sense of futility, a need to simply turn around and pretend no one else is here in the room with him. How well it would be just to sit down in his familiar chair with its tall, padded back and comfortable, worn elbow rests and direct his gaze to a motionless object before him. Maybe something with yellowing parchment and crumbling pages, with smooth dark lines of symbols rendered in cursive. Follow the curving script into a trance, embark into a bright place of meaning. . . .

But no, she is still here.

"Come now, aren't you going to ask me more about her?" Lady Izelle says. "About Nairis?"

He asks instead, "Where is that accursed merchant, the filth who brought this thing inside and then dared threaten me? Is he at least gone? What did he really want?"

Izelle shrugs. "Oh, he's gone. And he wanted only one thing—to be paid. What else? And so I paid him, freeing her from his vulgar clutches. She is but some poor bones, now. But she also happens to be a deceased ancient beauty and heiress. Small wonder the merchant thought there was some worth to be gained. At first he was trying to have her revived, supposedly by means of your secret powers. Then he was willing to just sell her off in whatever condition."

The Duke stares with incomprehension.

"Indeed," she says. "How very odd of him—to think of secret powers, of all things." And a smile engages the rosebud mouth, serving to irritate and yet somehow to beguile. "In any case, as you yourself surmised, m'Lord, she's my means of blackmailing you. Not only have you proved how much the relic sickens you, but on my way in I happened to overhear your man Harmion speak of your peculiar and pronounced dislike—and I stress the word *dislike*—of dead things."

"Why, my Lady, you really are despicable," says the Duke, taking a step toward her. His stance is aggressive. He has been frozen all through their conversation, and suddenly he is on the move. The light from the window suffuses the fine edges of his hair with violet, while the line of his silhouette is drawn in gold.

"If you must, I don't hate *her* half as much as you think," he says softly. "I don't dislike or fear death any more than does any man. What I do is exaggerate my distaste considerably for the sake of unwelcome visitors such as yourself. Don't presume for a moment that your blackmail will succeed. Because I'm about to have you thrown out before you say another word."

"You *don't* hate her? Really?"

She snatches the box from its place on the cluttered table and thrusts it almost in his face.

Rossian gasps, quickly attempts to stand back, his expression filling with recoil.

"Don't, please. . . ." He speaks in a faint voice, for in that moment it seems he is robbed of lung capacity by an ancient pneumonia. He raises one hand, as though to summon Harmion, anyone, then breathes in a deep shudder, and is miraculously once again composed.

"Why?" she persists, standing so close to him, holding the infernal box between them as a shield, or maybe a sword. "Is it because it has something to do with your sorcerous powers? Your *secret?* I knew it! Come, tell me—speak!"

"No," he says, straightening. "Because it smells like old mold."

And then a sad smile of resignation comes to his lips. "My Lady, would you join me for dinner?"

৩৩ II ৪৩ৰ

Things Somewhat More Serious

Early dinner is served in the great Hall of Violet. It is a cavernous place, beautiful as a thing of antiquity, for it too is crumbling, and repellent as a den of decay. Everything—from the great arched vault of the ceiling, the decorated frieze, the upswept pillars, and the decrepit linen tablecloth draping the long ancient table, down to the stones of the walls themselves—is in tones of purple, lavender, heliotrope, lilac, violet. Even the wine poured in their goblets by the liveried servants has a rich glint of plum and lilac when the candlelight falls on it. Candlelight is fierce and plentiful, for the Duke enjoys seeing his food and watching the play of fire upon glass and crystal surfaces, such as the chandelier that is suspended over the centerpoint of the long table in a cloud of radiance.

They dine alone. Rossian, having resigned himself to the intrusion, is now in a mood of apathy. It is his definitive condition, a state of suspended will, an abdication of being and strife. For the duration of the meal he will merely occupy his place in the room, nothing more.

He has changed into expensive near-black formal Ducal attire. If the Lady Izelle thinks he is formal and imposing in the tiny room earlier, she must now be overwhelmed by his glamour. Rings glitter on his fingers; each finger, an artwork of chiseled elegance. His throat is embraced by a cravat of lace. His cheeks, newly clean-shaven, reveal poetic hollows. His hair is smoothed into a faultless sheen, so that each strand lies next to the others blending in an illusion of a metal surface; the hair is gathered behind him into a queue, unpowdered and glinting burnished gold. His brows are almost straight and perfect, and as such lend his face an impassive authority, just as certain sounds in nature—the major C note—convey inviolate balance.

His eyes are averted as he focuses on the parade of succulent courses in front of him, and thus avoids interaction with her, for the most part. There is deliberate silence as he indulges in bites of pheasant soaked in a buttery wine sauce, followed by the tender breastmeat of another game infused with herbs and smothered in layers of quivering Gruyere and flaky pastry. Next comes duck drowned in its own juice amid mushroom splendor, dollops of cream sauce riding on a bed of aromatic grains, breads and puddings, and for dessert, glazed pears floating in shallow lagoons of raisin honey and rose-water.

Izelle has taken off her ugly pea-green cap with its cornucopia of useless embellishments. The cap now reposes on the table at her side, in a hideous parody of a served-up dish, and the decorous servants cast sidelong glances at it as they make their rounds. She has revealed short roughly trimmed dark hair, as though sheared off by a blunt implement in the hands of an unskilled child. Her hair glistens with deep plum highlights in the hall of Violet, for it cannot help but take on some of the predominant hue in this light. It lies in wisps and occasional curls, and gives her doll-face the charm of a much-handled beloved toy.

"Tell me," the Duke opens his mouth at some point, making indifferent small-talk, "do you always wear—*that*? And what about your House colors?"

She counters him with a look of unpleasant familiarity, spearing a buttery chunk of pastry with a slim knife and twirling it in the air before finally capsizing it between the rosebud lips. Her lips glisten with oily juices and she licks them with the tip of the tongue in a delicate gesture, innocent despite potential implications.

"And what about yours? Why the black, are you in mourning?"

His left brow rises. There is a shadow of amusement. "Not at all, unless you consider mourning to imply my everpresent dreary existence . . . no. Look closer. Not black—it is the deepest violet, so rich that the color almost dissipates into night. I am attired in my Colors. I embrace them, indeed—look 'round you."

"Ah, then. I am nearsighted somewhat. Forgive my blindness, my Lord. You are undeniable in your Violet."

A pause as they simultaneously raise goblets to drink another fine aged vintage from the Duke's cellars.

He waits while his glass is refilled, says, "What of the Duchess, what is she like? And does she always wear White?"

Izelle removes from her neck the bulky chain with the locket. He watches her child-sized fingers move, soft and slim, as she handles the pendant.

"Here, see for yourself. My Cousin is virginally White."

She reaches forward, hands her treasure to a nearby

servant, who takes it formally and delivers across the table.

The Duke opens the silver clasp. Inside, two great eyes greet him from a frill of white snow gauze and veils. "A remarkable resemblance," he says, after a thoughtful moment. "If I didn't know for a fact that she is imprisoned in her own home just as myself, I would say that she is you."

Lady Izelle smiles. "Maybe I *am* she. Would that surprise you, my Lord? A mystery unfolds before you, suddenly. The Duchess has sprung her prison and is here in person, before you. In truth, miracles happen, as you know. What do you say to that?"

"Nothing, for I must first think upon it," he says, raising the wine to his lips which are neither overly full nor austere. They are such that could sneer and smile in one movement, and which can appear cruel-set or warm and sensual depending on the expression of the face, the grand whole. They are a perfect set of lips for a diplomat whose main advantage is the veneer of neutrality.

"So, tell me, Lady Izelle, are you, then, the Duchess of White? Come, admit it, and then explain," he mocks. He has gone on the offensive, and now questions her with the intent to bait.

Izelle looks at the spot on the tablecloth where a dish of pastry has just been removed by a servant, and there is a moist circle and a spot with crumbs. She is waiting, being coy.

"I would never want to be in her place," she says at last. "Besides, she is quite plain, isn't she? Plain Jane. That's her name, too."

And with those words Izelle looks up, looking directly into his distant eyes.

The Duke examines the locket.

"Plain? Somewhat . . ." he says. "Except, her eyes are

intense and astute. Which makes her interesting as opposed to merely ordinary—somewhat like you."

"And is this where you decide to be kind to me, or are we still engaged in mockery, m'Lord? I'm afraid I wouldn't know the difference anymore," she says softly; as if she ever did. "I don't particularly like such comments. They are said for the wrong reasons, always."

He laughs. It is a deep warm sound, yet complex like one of his wines.

"What, are you suggesting that I'm giving you a cheap indirect compliment? Rest assured, no. Besides, if you weren't my guest, I'd tell you the truth—I find you quite unattractive."

He speaks this suddenly in an icy tone, and his expression is hard, while he watches her closely. "But then, you really *aren't* a guest, is it not so? I almost forgot. Our dinner was being so pleasant, as long as one didn't . . . think too closely."

The Lady Izelle stares at him as though he is drunk, which at this point in the dining journey he most commonly is. Though, is he, this time, tonight? It is something she will never know.

"Madam—Lady—whatever you are, cousin of my distant relation, or the blessed Duchess herself. You are forcefully making yourself into a guest when you're not at all welcome. So I needn't hold back at all. It's in my power to insult you; indeed, it is my duty. There. . . . You, my dear, are quite ugly. And you can tell it to your Duchess too, if indeed the two of you comprise two separate individuals. She is just like you. Or you are just like her. Or whichever."

Izelle's eyes are a surprise. Honest for once, with a peculiar clarity. "Thank you," she says. "For being so straightforward with me." If such a thing were possible, she appears animated rather than perturbed by the put-down.

"Oh, with torpid pleasure." He motions away tiredly with his hand as a servant offers yet another dessert. "I was even more charming with the Duchess of Red. I told her annoying chit of a second nephew's sister that from the grotesque picture she presented to me, her complexion was quite befitting her House colors. In particular, Her Grace's bulb nose."

Izelle chokes, then raises her palm to cover her mouth. Even then, in that uttermost cliché of a gesture, she is not being coy, because she follows up with a nasal goose-honk.

The Duke's left brow begins to rise.

"That's what I thought too," she explains. "Only I never told her minion that—after all, my Cousin, the Duchess, would not have approved."

She pauses suddenly, growing serious; the winged messenger of the gods has nothing on her ability to shift moods. "You know, Your Grace, you truly *are* cruel. I don't mean amusing rudeness and sarcasm, I mean—You speak the exact truth. It might be because you have been so innocent of human interaction for so long, locked up here among the stones and the arcane books, with only servants to keep you company. You are very much alone, am I wrong? Solitude can leech away all social subtleties and make one heartless. Maybe I shouldn't blame you, really, but—no matter. At least I don't think I am like that, thank heaven."

In a sharp movement she jumps up, nearly upending her chair, startling the nearest servant into a wobbling hold on his laden tray. "You know what, Rossian?—"

"First of all, don't call me that."

"But your name is—"

"Don't. It is vulgar. And it is not my proper name where you are concerned. I am Rossian, but you have not earned this familiarity."

"Oh, poppycock! Well, then, *my Lord*, Your High and Mighty Grace who abhors vulgarity, let's, out of nothing else to do, have a contest!"

"What? And who says I have nothing else to do?"

She stands at her place setting, then snatches up the monstrous cap and puts it back on her head again, askew, and her face is nearly obscured with the flamboyant rodent's nest. As he watches from his seat, mildly amused at this sideshow and filled with an equal measure of annoyance, she leans forward, baring her pretty teeth in excitement, possibly in a kind of manic expression of anger.

"Let us," she says, "have a little contest of power. Just a *little* tiny small one. And in lieu of the prize, the loser shall tell the other his or her secret, swearing to its truthfulness."

"What?" His genuine annoyance and surprise grow, and he too is suffused with anger.

"I said, I challenge you to it. Or, more properly put, my Cousin challenges you by proxy. A game! What marvelous distraction and fun, my Lord. Think of it as something to take away your endless hours of tedium, something to occupy you, a game of sorcery and power!"

"Are you serious?" he says, beginning to rise out of his seat. "Are you versed in the arts enough to defy me? And what makes you think I'll give away the secret even if I lose, or that I would trust *you* to give your Cousin's?"

"We will swear . . . a great Oath."

"Hah!" he says, settling back once more. "I don't swear."

"But we could!"

"Come now, don't be a fool more than you already are. We are simply sitting here eating dinner. I'd like to have some peace. Besides, I don't trust you. Why should I?"

"Why not? What's there to lose? You are bored. You are

dying. And maybe, here you have the chance to gain a secret for your arsenal."

"I am . . . dying . . ." he whispers to himself, suddenly feeling his head go cold. While servants continue moving about the hall, while candlelight casts its warm even glow and the crystals on the chandelier sparkle as in moments before, he enters a strange detached semi-dream state from which he observes things through layers of cotton. He is swaddled by something in the air of the room, and it is stifling him.

The Duke speaks, finally. "Yes, how did you. . . ?"

"I knew it from the beginning. From the way your castle appears. At dinner, you never asked me for news of the outside world. You wear deep Violet, but not for the reasons that may be on the surface, not for your House. It is, in fact, an approximation of darkness, of mourning—for yourself."

"I am dying . . ." he repeats.

"Yes, as Jane is . . . As all of them. The Dukes are dying, because their souls are caged. It's eating away, like rust. Maybe it's true that from the moment we come out of the womb we are all dying as mortals do, but with the Dukes, it's a stagnant moldering death, a conscious one. A pool of water with no inflow, cut off from its original supply, begins to grow foul before it evaporates, breeding mosquitoes and disease. Long before the water is gone from the standing pool, it is not fit to drink."

His eyes are dark with widened pupils, violet, black. He looks at her, then glances at a far window, where the multi-colored sky shows the sun beginning to set. "I envy you . . ." he whispers. "You, who are free and not one of us."

"Then you must learn my Cousin's secret. And then the others. So, swear!"

"The holiest Oath? No."

"Yes . . . that one, why not. And I will also."

"Oh. . . ."

The Duke feels something begin to move inside him, a familiar pull, the same restless urge that he has learned over the years to rein in, to stifle with complacency and the illusion of serene occupation. The call is like a fly caught in a jar; it beats against the glass, buzzing in fury, then settles for a moment in infinite stillness, then begins to struggle again. Such is rebellion—not a single act but a series of bursts and refractory periods that together comprise a pattern of directed *change*.

The Duke realizes that his own pattern is calling to him, calling him to initiate its making. Liberty is on the other side of the glass jar, and he merely needs to beat against the glass— relentlessly, periodically, occasionally, even just once—until he either comes forth in a paroxysm on the other side or dies.

The other side is so close. . . . If he stands at the castle courtyard, at the edges of the gates (he has done so, many times), he can breathe the air flavored by it, air that pours at him from the free outside, past the invisible enclosure.

With a wrench, the Duke takes his thoughts out of the stream of familiar longing and directs himself to stand up.

The servants attend him immediately, hurrying to open doors for his exit while others begin to clear the table. And yet, he merely stands, his gaze directed at the child-woman across from him, and they watch each other, already engaged in a contest of sorts.

"How shall we swear?" the Duke says.

And Izelle's rosebud mouth warms into curvature, for she has already won.

She approaches him. The world is suddenly dreamlike in the way of the bizarre, with Izelle pulling out her long knife (it's tucked at her belt, screaming of smoky kitchens with soot-covered walls and brick ovens). First she bares the wrist by pulling up her voluminous shirtsleeve and doublet below which her arms are skinny sticks. Then she uses the point of the knife to draw a bead of blood from her wrist. In the moment of piercing skin she is fearless. The blood wells immediately, an angry little poinsettia berry against the Dresden pale skin.

She passes the knife on to Duke Rossian, who watches her in surprise. Up to this moment he does not believe in the reality of what's unfolding, but the blood is so final; blood is always real—which makes him serious and solemn. If he pays attention he can hear the rush in his own veins and arteries, the circulation and the clockwork pump underlying all movement. While in the distance, above, below, he senses the echo of subterranean waters and sky waters. They comprise the outside world.

The Duke takes the knife, pulls up his lace-trimmed sleeve, and proceeds to do the same to his own white flesh. There is a moment of dull unexpected pain, for the knife tip is more blunt than he thinks.

And then his own blue blood comes forth crimson. He watches the inside of his wrist, strong and graceful, and stained with the red. He has been careful not to prick a vein, but the blood seems unwilling to be contained and now he is frightened for a moment of his own vigor, of what he has done—slit his own wrist, by heaven!—and for what?

But before he has another moment to be consumed by doubt, Izelle moves her own bloodied wrist with its perfectly round globule specimen of life-juice, and with an odd beastlike cry (its nature is half-forgotten, but sends shivers through them both), she presses their hands together at eye level between them (he leans down from his height to meet her), wrist to wrist, controlled blood drop to exuberant blood smear.

There is a mingling of pulse-beat. The Duke knows her own smaller, quicker, lighter clockwork mechanism through the contact of wrist to wrist, past the skin. In that mingling he also knows the bellows of her lungs and the churning of her bones in their sockets of tendon and flesh, the fierce glow in her womb, her odd corresponding fire of *animus* that sits in warm slow simmer at her solar plexus, her blazing other center past her throat and, higher up, the suddenly gaping twilight place in the maw of her skull—

Something pulls him back violently, and he is made aware that he has seen too far inside her, must not know any more, and that she is dangerous. It happens in a blink, of course, or even a span less, a fractured space between heartbeats. And then the contact is broken, and he is himself, and now his wrist is stinging, stained with their common blood.

She is breathing fast, watching him, and he can almost sense the bond drawn in a line between them, from her wrist to his, and the expectant pause, also strung in the air.

"I swear," he says in a faint voice.

"I swear," she echoes.

"We are kin." They complete the oath together.

And for the duration of their deal, even if all this is nonsense, they are now bound.

The Duke feels the peculiar urge to chortle and cry out, to hyperventilate, and something in the expression of her eyes tells him she is equally wound, although neither would admit to it. They are sudden children at the brink of engaging in a forbidden act.

"And now," Izelle exclaims, "we can play!" She claps her hands together, ignoring the wrist upon which the blood has already began to coagulate and heal, and the white linen shirtsleeve is lightly stained in sprinkles of red as it slips back down. . . .

"What are the rules?" he asks, tense as a string. "Who'll decide the rules? Shall I?"

"I suppose it would only be fitting if you did," she replies. "Considering you have graciously agreed to my idea."

Rossian thinks that grace has nothing to do with it. *Why am I doing this anyway? Why, really? This is idiot insanity.* His instinct of suspicion reaches out, nerves pulling at others in bundles individually it seems, a delicate agonized state of alertness, of tingling knowledge in every cell of his skin. But his blood is racing now, and he does not want to stop himself, because for the first time since he can remember, he is feeling fiercely *alive.* . . .

"I can read your thoughts, you know," she says, clearly taunting him.

"Then the first rule is, you'll do none of that!" he exclaims in a suddenly harsh voice without a blink of surprise and begins walking out of the hall. "And neither will I. I do not—*pry*. We, both of us, will not pry into minds." Each word he speaks now is strongly punctuated, distinct, like a weapon thrown.

His strides are long and she is startled into keeping up, half-running behind him as they move through the large open space via double doors of mahogany, into a smaller elongated chamber that has a number of chairs lining the walls and decrepit ancestral portraits hung above each, the oils having dulled and the varnish yellowed into an overall tone of funereal brown. The servants stand aside as the Duke passes, then light the tapers in the wall sconces and disappear discreetly, one after another, with the last closing the doors to the grand hall behind them.

If you could read my mind, he thinks, *we wouldn't be*

doing this now, this pretense. Although, I myself am to blame. I want to do it, I now realize. My blood quickens . . . My blood. Maybe all of this is my doing.

He stops in the middle of the chamber and she follows suit. She stands before him, hands clutched together, rubbing palms unconsciously, her forehead and brows moving in nervous reflex. "Agreed. What else, my Lord?"

"What else? Why, the rest of the rules, of course," Rossian says. In a peculiar reaction to his own outburst, his perfect face has loosened with sensuality and he is on the verge of smiling in anticipation. There is quirky pleasure to be gained by such word play as now, and he allows himself to take advantage of the moment. "How shall we go about it, my Lady Izelle? Do you recall Hide and Seek, that children's game you might have played when you were a tot, or whatever the urchins call it? We will borrow the rules and make them our own. Our game will be identical. Except, *acts* of power are added."

She gasps, in equal semblance of pleasure. "Of course! How very silly and simple and clever of you, my Lord, a game with so many possibilities."

"I'll do you the courtesy of allowing you the first move."

She smiles lightly inclining her head. "So generous."

The Duke decides there is an undertone of sarcasm. But he is so eager to begin that he is beyond fine analysis or regret.

"Hide," he says. "Hide anywhere within the grounds of my castle. In any *way* you can. And if, within the duration of ten minutes, according to this timepiece—" he points to a corner cabinet grandfather clock with carved molding and a small hourglass insert that floats in a recessed niche built precisely for it, an unusual one-of-a-kind piece—"I am unable to find you, then you win the round."

"Marvelous!" she exclaims. "When may I hide?"

"Now," he replies. He walks to the cabinet, reaches forward with his elegant hand and turns the tiny sand-filled glass within its niche. Then he inhales deeply and shuts his eyes for the sake of proper courtesy, knowing intuitively it is not quite necessary.

For, the next second he opens them, she is gone.

Rossian glances once about the hall of portraits, and there is resounding silence. The long runner carpet of Turkish wool covers the crude wooden slats of floor like a faded peacock's tail. The slim candles flicker alongside the walls and cast parabolic effusions of light upon the oils; the deeply carved patterns on the old gilded frames are cast in sharp relief. He senses the breathing of ancestral ghosts as they reside in the walls between the slabs of granite, and fill the air with a permanent sense of someone else's memory just out of reach.

The clock in the corner reclaims his attention, for now it is the only source of movement in the room. In the niche the sand falls from one glass compartment to the other while above it the rounded face of the clock stares like a sleeping moon, and the hands move in stately microscopic precision. Just below, the brass pendulum swings with a clean rhythmic click to mark the seconds.

The Duke watches the clockface and the polished wood of the cabinet and the pendulum and the thin stream of the flowing sand.

And then he laughs, a patrician arrogant sound. "Oh, come now, you insult my capabilities. Come out, my dear. Come out of the little glass chamber, before you drown like a fly in the running sand—which might not be such a regrettable thing at all, considering it would rid me of you."

One blink of the eye, and the shapes of the room waver in his vision like objects seen through heated air before a furnace, a desert mirage, and Izelle again stands before him in her tasteless attire.

"Really," he says. "Couldn't you be a little more ingenious? We've decided upon ten minutes, not ten seconds."

She smiles lightly, as though not hearing the sarcasm. "I was testing the deep waters. The depth of you."

He snorts. "More likely, deep sand. Shall we disregard this then and start again?" His tone is polite, even. Within, his blood pounds.

"Oh, no, no. By all means count it as part of the round. Your turn."

"Very well, although I must say, an odd decision on your part to relinquish this opportunity. And now, don't even bother to close your eyes, simply mark the time."

But she is already before the clock cabinet, turning the glass nodule with its sand in the other direction, allowing the few seconds of time that has elapsed in the first round to be returned back to origin. "It is done."

And then she turns the glass again, and time resumes.

He responds by inclining his head in a mock bow, and then he is not there.

Sorcery has unfurled, and it is now rampant in the castle. If one can only sense it, there is a clamor of force in the air, and the stones acquire lungs, pumping the breath of life to animate them. Everything resonates underneath the surface. Even the dust motes are primed to take off and swirl with more energy than normal, in secret opposition to the air currents.

If one can sense it.

Izelle gives a big sigh, whether in relief or resignation, is unclear. It is also unclear what, if anything, she can perceive happening in the metasphere around her. She shrugs to herself, then carelessly starts looking about.

She does not tarry in the hall of portraits but quickly walks the length of the carpet to the great carved doors on the side opposite that of the Hall of Violet. She pushes against the smooth wood with one petite hand and is in the hallway. Here she stops the butler, Harmion who is waiting, and now exhibits the same sort of distaste for her presence as his master. He carries a single candle in a polished brass holder that has the odd shape simultaneously reminiscent of a Dutch clog shoe and an Arabian Evenings Aladdin's lamp.

"Where is my box?" she asks, staring at him with the intensity of a vulture.

"M'Lady?" The man's one greying brow artfully rises in a dissonant combination of barely concealed horror and civility as he attempts to edge away from her without dripping hot candle wax upon his gnarled fingers.

"The box with the remains, I mean. Do you recall our conversation regarding a certain ancient beauty, possibly irrelevant to all of this, or possibly not? Nairis the Fabled One? My means of Ducal blackmail?"

"How could one forget. . . ."

"Where is my Lord the Duke, by the way?"

"Most probably in his study. Would you like your—ahem—*box*, now? Would you, perchance be considering a departure?"

"Almost, my good man. First, the box, and then our Duke. Or rather, first the Duke, and the box will ensue, reasserting itself."

"As you wish."

She follows Harmion and his solitary candle down several corridors, stopping before a somewhat familiar door.

"His study," says the butler. I believe the *thing* you inquire about is within."

"The Duke is within? Oh, good."

"His Grace is not a thing. I refer to the remains of Nairis. And His Grace might also be present. Shall I inquire—"

"No, thank you. And—do you have a sense of play?" she suddenly adds, watching with amusement.

"Only with my Lord I do. For others, only sarcasm," Harmion responds with dignity, and turns away, disdaining another word.

"Stop," she says. "Come closer, yes, here. Now put that candle down on the side table here, yes. No, do not stare at me so, just do as I ask, please."

Frowning, the butler obeys. The candle holder is deposited with tremulous arthritic hands upon a narrow table in the corridor.

"Now walk. Back and forth in the patch of candlelight."

Harmion stares at her for once as though she is genuinely addled. And then he slowly begins to pace where she indicates, while she in turn watches him.

"That will be enough, Harmion, thank you."

"Anything else. . . ?" At this point he is prepared to be unsurprised if she requests him to stand on his head.

"Yes," she says. "Duke Rossian, come out of his shadow." And without looking back, she enters the study. Rossian steps within immediately behind her.

Inside the room, the single observation window with its well-worn elbow ledge shows the sun fading in a red coal sliver at the horizon. Air pours with cold into the chamber, while the sky is a mass of indigo twilight and splotches of rust. Soon, the shutters will need to be drawn for the night.

"Not too bad," he says. "Only four minutes and a dozen seconds. However, as a proxy of your Cousin, you have lost the round."

She stands with her back to him, a silhouette against the fading light. "I did, didn't I."

It is the strangest thing she has said yet.

For one instant Rossian almost feels sorry for her, but the feeling is supplanted by wary confusion. "My Lady, you are so very peculiar," he says in a blank voice. "Why? What is this, all of this, really for you? What kind of game are you playing with me? You practically set yourself up for defeat, and I am unsure why. I don't understand you—though, only moments ago I thought I did—and it's making me disillusioned about our game. Is that what you want? Or have you been sent here by your Duchess to drive me insane with uncertainty?"

He pauses, watching her for any reaction, but she still has not moved, standing with her back to him, which is unnerving.

"Well, then," he continues. "I say we call it a foul and start again. My sense of justice does not allow me to take such an advantage of you—even if you *are* an annoyance, or even a malicious Ducal toad."

Izelle turns at last, to look at him. Her mutable eyes are an unsolved puzzle in the semi-dark. "Don't you want to find out my Cousin's secret?" she asks earnestly. She does not blink, or at least he does not see a movement, for the room has grown too dark.

"Not in particular . . . I would rather simply play." His response is in turn more earnest than he wants to admit. It simply comes out of him as an exhalation of breath. Words laden with twilight.

His manner is suddenly exhausted, apathetic in the usual way, and inside him the game is over. Out there, beyond the window, the sky has turned into a pit of darkness. The sun is gone. The room is now a morass thrown into interminable gloom.

"Harmion!" he calls without using the bell pull, as though the old butler has preternatural senses and can hear him—mayhap he does, lurking patiently outside his door. "Harmion, some light here! A candle, please."

"That's all you want, isn't it, to play? Why don't you care the same way as all the rest of them?" Izelle says. "I thought you were dying because you couldn't be free."

"I am . . . tired. Of futility."

"But you never even tried! Not as the others try, constantly!"

Harmion enters, his candle flickering, shadows swinging wildly. He does not need to be told and approaches the work table with its dust-strewn clutter of books, and finds the oil lamp. The candle dips precariously into the open neck, makes contact, and the wick inside catches on fire. With a spark the lamp ignites, and the glow it casts around the room is full and rich, unlike the small elemental flicker of the candle.

Next, Harmion proceeds to close the shutters, and the cold from the outside is now kept out, contained.

There is enough cold left within this room—cold expressions, cold words, cold beating clockwork of hearts, fueled with frustrated anger.

"It is precisely why I stopped trying," the Duke says. "Because I see them thus, so despicable and vulgar, so desperately selfish, coming here trying to wheedle this thing out of me. I am not like them. I may be selfish and wicked but at least I'm not a vulture."

Harmion exits, closing the door soundlessly behind him.

Izelle sighs. She walks to the table where the infamous box with the remains of Nairis stands as it has been originally placed. She ignores it and instead watches the lamp, its steady orange glow that suffuses the room. It is the only source of warmth.

She inhales deeply the air that has received a fragrant effusion of the lamp oil. The scent is a pleasing mixture of roses and wild sage.

"Then—why don't you simply *tell* them—tell me!—what the essence of your secret is, out of plain mercy?" she whispers. "*You* at least, could be noble where they would not."

"I don't have mercy for them. They are obscene, dirt. Besides, it would make no difference."

"I suppose that makes me dirt also."

She looks at him, searches for any reaction.

The Duke pulls up his chair and sits down. He puts one foot up over the other, folds his arms in a stubbornly comfortable pose. His beautiful face limned with golden glow is impassive.

"Well, then," she carries on. "I don't think we should continue this game."

"I thought we were done playing some time ago."

But she ignores his matter-of-fact sarcasm, his veneer of boredom. "Since in the name of the Duchess I have lost, it would only be fair that I tell you her secret now, as we've agreed."

"You what?"

The Duke is immobilized. Even his breath fades, and for a moment he is a dead thing bereft of existence. And then he allows his lungs to resume their cycle, to expand and billow with life-breath, while his heartbeat is marking time.

"Why are you doing this?" he says. "Enough with your contortions and sleight of mouth. What exactly do you *want*?"

She shrugs. "Answer my question first: do you care to find out the secret power of the Duchess of White? Would you like to *know,* my Lord?"

He stares, and an indescribable thing appears in his

expression; he is transfigured and cast far away from here; he is vacant and wandering in a place of hope, and is living in a different moment than she. "No," he says at last. "I actually don't want to know. I don't care what the devil it is, not a whit."

"Then why are you so unwilling to part with your own secret?" she exclaims.

"Because, damn you, I don't *have* one!"

Silence. They stare at one another.

"Yes . . ." he says then, quietly. "My grand secret is that I don't have a secret. At least not one of which I am aware. And neither was my father—or any other blessed ancestor—aware of any secret power, only of being senselessly imprisoned within this hateful place."

Izelle exhales. "Oh. . . ."

And now the Duke gets up and begins to pace restlessly, knocking his chair out of the way with one angry movement of his foot.

"Well? How do you like my revelation, my Lady?" he says, spitting the words out. "Like it or not, it is a fact. We have all tried to take a step outside the gates countless years, countless number of times, yet—there is *something* out there, something preventing us, every time. Unlike our supposed powers, it is a genuine physical force, it is *real* and hard and strong. I've tried myself, repeatedly, and—" He throws up a hand in resignation.

"How did it feel?" she asks, speaking in an odd manner while looking ahead of herself, not at him. "How did it *feel* when you tried to *pass* the boundary?"

"How? It felt like hell's bowels; always does. At first, there's an iron wall invisibly pressing, and yet molding against you somehow—not as true metal but as something that's similarly firm and cold and smooth—and this something does not allow you any further movement. And then, if you press on further, struggle against it—as I've done—there's a sort of darkness. And then your will and your mind goes blank."

"And then?"

"That's all. I've found myself losing consciousness every time, and waking up lying on the ground, within the boundary of the castle. Either that, or Harmion would drag me off to bed, and when I came to, would hover over me with the physician, the two of them fussing like a pair of laying hens."

He grows silent, for there is little else to say. Then he sits down again on his chair, first moving it away from the work table, away from her, into the corner of the room.

He closes his eyes. Moments line up into armies and pass by in regimental regularity. The oil lamp continues to cast its warm glow, beginning to smoke slightly when a tiny flying insect enters the top of its neck, flitters, and eventually capsizes in hot lipid death.

"Will you please leave now?" he says softly, turning away from her, from everything. "Now that you have what you came for. I've told you the truth. I've sworn to it, haven't I? Despite the fact that I won the imbecile round of an imbecile game of ours, and you lost, I've told you. Because—for a few moments, I must admit—you've given me a reason to breathe, and entertained me with a children's game. I've never really— *played* with anyone in such a way. Thank you."

And then he lets himself sink, submerging into a kind of separate private consciousness, locking the world away, not caring for anything, unaware of his own body, except for the dark waves of depression; it is entering him at each psychic opening, coming up from the nether places in the earth that run deep beneath the castle. . . .

Except that when next he becomes aware of the

surroundings, coming to himself who knows how long afterwards, *she* is still there, standing small and grotesque a few feet away.

The candlelight seeps in an even glow from behind her silhouette, a halo of a saint who's stepped out from one of the tapestries—except the bright corona encompasses all of her.

And in that glow, she approaches.

She draws near; is leaning to watch him, serious and *different* (something new is indeed there; he has never yet seen this beatific aspect of her), and her eyes are liquid with compassion.

And in that, she is terrifying.

"Rossian . . ." she whispers.

"What? Still here?" he says harshly, straightening in his chair. "My Lady Izelle, has *anyone* taught you common courtesy, ever? I told you, I *told* you the truth! Now, begone, little demon! I've even thanked you—hah!—thanked you for sickening and annoying me in a novel way, unlike those other Ducal dullards, to the extent of actually bringing me enjoyment, an odd moment or two—"

"Coming from you, it is complimentary, I suppose." She speaks matter-of-factly, still leaning over him, her unearthly gaze never leaving his face. And then she says something else, a thing so deep and serious that breath catches in his throat.

"What would you say to me if I showed you a way of escaping your ageless prison?"

"You *what?*" he whispers. He is completely stricken, and rendered inarticulate.

"You don't believe me, do you? That it can be done? That a Ducal Heir can simply get up, completely resolved to accomplish it, and walk out of his or her castle? Well, Sir, it has been done, already. A certain Duchess of White decided she's had enough, plainly disgusted with her lot. And so she just walked through the gates, and out of her land.

"That Duchess is I, my Lord, as you might've already guessed in a moment of clarity. I am Janerizel of White. And I've come here to help you."

He stares at her coldly, unblinking, and then mutters. "I knew there was something fishy about you, something not quite right, that stank of deception and tomfoolery. Why didn't you simply tell me all of this in the first place, why all the lies? What *am* I supposed to believe?"

Her rosebud mouth curves into a little sad smile. "Ah, my Lord, a Duchess alone has to be careful. But then so are you—careful and alone. Indeed, it's always this way, isn't it? Never trust a soul. This way, even now, you'll not be a bit surprised."

"Of course not," he says. "I wouldn't be surprised until I believed you. And how can I? You claim impossible nonsense."

"It is *not* nonsense! I am the Duchess of White, you fool, idiot and imbecile! Mistrusting, dry-souled wretch! A frog in your own swampy filth is what you are, decaying and rotting in this blue blood hole! I am *here*, in your castle, and how do you think I got here?"

The saint has gone and in her place is a harridan who is screaming in his face, bits of her spittle striking him in an oddly intimate manner, so that he feels it on his cheeks, feels it coming from her doll's mouth. Tiny living projectiles, from her to him.

She moves away from him then, furious, her eyes attaining a mad quality, dilated and intense.

"I don't know," he says, his lips trembling from the effort to contain an involuntary smile. "You should've been forthright with me from the beginning. Why else all this foolery on your part? You could still be pretending, on behalf of your

Cousin, in order to get some other non-existent but suspected information out of me—"

"I don't *have* a cousin! I made her up! Lies, all I've told you! I am the Jane I told you about, and I'm Izelle. Both are me. Jane is when I'm ordinary and everyday-dull. Izelle is when I feel alive."

"And this is feeling alive? Fair enough," he says, rearranging himself in his seat yet again. "Supposing you really are the Duchess (an exotic fool, more like), how the devil did you escape? And why come help me?"

"Infernal questions," she says. "Why can't you simply believe me—" and then, pauses. "What am I saying? If I were in your place, I'd not believe such a lunatic as myself either, not for anything, no. . . ."

"How did you escape?" he repeats, his tone neutral, so as not to startle her out of whatever possible wondrous thing she is about to tell him. He is alert, waiting.

The Duchess of White begins to pace. "The very first unexpected thing to happen was that I found out my secret."

The Duke watches her, listening with all his being, and yet on another level he is busy reconciling the details of her with the reality; Duchess is a chit in a jester costume, with a face like a toy and the lips of a doll, and the manner of a madwoman. He is in the same room with another genuine blue blood of the realm, inside his very own castle! She is here, and she has broken free of the curse, somehow! Or . . . he could be dreaming. Or, even worse, this is all a malicious lie, the perpetuation of some dark charade. . . .

Izelle continues. "Once I found out the secret, all else followed. Yes, now you are surprised, I can see. But it's true. Just as you, I didn't know it either, the so-called secret power of White. Indeed, I suspect that at first none of the Dukes are aware of their power, having to discover it as I have. It's the process in which lies the key."

"What is your secret?" he asks, in genuine innocence.

Enough, he wants to scream, *tell me, tell me, tell me!*

Her gaze is elsewhere, doesn't meet his. "Since I've lost in our little silly game, since I've forced myself into your noble company and tormented you all day, I owe you the truth. And so I'll tell you everything—but in due time. First, *your* secret. You see, I am helping you and not just any other Ducal offspring, for a rather selfish reason: I *need* you. Your sorcerous power is the only thing that can help—"

She cuts off her words. It's as though she is afraid to proceed.

He gets up, beginning to say "But I have no power," then says instead: "What significance is there in my knowing my secret power, Duchess?"

"I think . . . when you gain an awareness of it, you will also have an awareness of the indescribable boundary that holds us all in. Knowing it, you will know how to transcend it."

Her words are abstract, yet accompanied by an expression so secure in knowledge, that for once Rossian, more doubting than the devil he so likes to invoke, thinks it prudent to believe her.

"What must I do?" he asks curtly.

Janerizel smiles at him. "You already know that I meddle with the arts . . . well then. Since I was informed by *sources* beyond this mortal coil that by its nature my secret bears a paradoxical relationship to yours, I was able to infer what your secret is. But—oh, what a truly heaven-decreed opportunity fell to me at the gates of your castle! When I saw that vendor of curiosities with his peculiar remains, I suppose it all fell into place at once—everything. And I'll explain it all, afterwards. I really will. . . .

"But first, you, my Lord, must overcome your natural disgust, as you call it, and do the humanly impossible. Bring Nairis the Fabled One back to life."

ೞೞ III ೞೞ
Deepening

They are in a small inner courtyard of the castle, this one a particularly isolated spot the size of a monk's cell, a narrow space between uninterrupted walls with only one decrepit entrance marked off by a swinging door of ancient wood mounted on rusty iron hinges. The purpose of this outer room open wide to the elements is unknown, buried in the past. Mayhap it once serves as an herb garden, a meeting room for secret lovers or conspirators, a place to isolate unruly children or to keep domesticated beasts and their feed troughs. Now, there is nothing here but beaten dirt for a floor, with possible slabs of stone buried deep underneath, with high walls that are looming above them on all four sides like mountains, engendering the illusion of being at the bottom of a well. There is but a patch of ink sky overhead, with several pinpoints of stars.

The butler, Harmion, directs servants to set up a narrow

long table and two chairs. No one is in the mood for sitting, however. The funeral box is placed on the tabletop which is covered by a long spread of chamois cloth, with two candles on both ends, sending tiny feeble light into the nighttime blackness. They are safe from high winds here, the candles and their droplet amber flames. Safe, yet oddly vulnerable to a possible wrath of sky. . . .

"Look, my Lord, no moon tonight . . ." Janerizel says, standing a little to the side. Her words are innocent.

"Really?" Rossian's voice is drenched in his customary cold sarcasm. "What is this thing, this moon? With so little empty sky in which I can look up, it's a rarity that I glimpse the moon, even if it is full."

"I suppose this is but one of the few places within your castle grounds where you get any open sky at all. Be grateful for that much—in my castle where I was imprisoned, I had no such courtyard. I *never* saw the sky, except out of a window."

Such a minor observation. And she does not speak bitterly at all. Yet he has to look at her nevertheless, seeing again an instant of pathos in her little figure, her wretched clothing (why does she wear it?), her childish eyes. Again, almost a twinge of pity.

In the meantime, servants depart, closing the heavy wooden door behind them, no doubt wondering at the newest madness of their Duke who is up to something ungodly in the middle of the night.

Rossian watches the last man leave. And then he walks slowly, his movement marking the perimeter of walls, the empty open *space* beyond which lies more stone, thick as the height of a man or maybe the span of an arm. He thinks of that massive span as he stretches out his hand to touch the wall, brushing fingers against it as he walks, to be repulsed initially by its wet slickness of moss and lichen in spots; stone perspiring everywhere, covered with cold moisture of the night air.

Izelle stands restless, seeming to feel his motion, to mark it; maybe she detects a faint gathering of power. She observes the thin elegant figure of Duke Rossian, and—could it be?—she might suddenly imagine him at the castle gates all those countless times, as he leans against the *air*, places his body in such a position that he could not be naturally supported, hand outthrust just as it is now, virtually resting against a wall of nothing. She might visualize him pushing while power bounces back and the unbreachable boundary holds, its metaphysical resonances like echoes in his mind. . . .

He lets go of the wall and steps away, turning to her. "Here we are. What comes next?"

"This. You must approach the box filled with death and focus upon it. Invoke your power and the extent of your arts, ponder what it is that you can do to revive her."

Revive her. . . . What right, to disturb ancient bones? he thinks suddenly. Doubt assails him—not doubt of his ability but doubt of purpose—and it fills him with momentary vertigo. *To pull her out of the eternal sleep into the dank and dreary here and now. And for what? What if she wants oblivion, what if she does not want to live? What if. . . .*

Rossian approaches the table. The dark is silent but for the humming of several night moths flying to the candle flames. He stands regarding the rectangular black, red and gold thing before him, wordless.

"Then it's true . . ." Janerizel says. "I can even now *sense* the turbulence of power, the aversion you feel for it, for the death within."

"Yes. . . ." His voice is a whisper. "I've never realized this before, not with all my learning and pursuit of the mysteries of power—truth is, I am naturally *repulsed* by death. Repulsed, in the way of sorcery. I've always made light of it, thinking myself to be but overly fastidious. . . ."

No, not repulsed, no. The bones sleep . . . so sweetly. Must they be woken? Let them be, oh let them be. . . .

"Touch it," she whispers in turn. "Open the box and place the remains before you on the table."

"I wonder who she was, this Nairis, when she lived. And how that merchant ever procured her, since supposedly she is blue blood—or was. It's strange, really. I can't think of any Ducal branch that would allow such a careless mockery of their deceased. I suspect that he or someone before him might've stolen her unfortunate bones—Only, how is that possible?"

"My Lord Rossian," she says, an unexpected hardness in her voice. "Stop stalling. You must do it. The night is cold, and your aversion will not lessen."

He throws her one look, his eyes narrowing from habit of disdain. Only, it is not disdain. If only she could know. . . .

And then slowly, with both hands, he reaches for the box.

It might be a trick of unsteady candlelight blown about by the softest gusts of wind from the spaces overhead, but there is something; strangeness is happening. A pearlescent glow, very faint, begins to envelop his hands. There is a delicate green tint to the whiteness, different from the yellow-gold candle glow, a hint of phosphor, swirling waves of mother-of-pearl. It gathers about his fingertips, noticeable only in contrast to the candle's golden hues, something that never would be apparent in daylight.

His hands start moving in the manner of a caress; they stroke the outside of the box for an instant only, brushing against worn wood (when only moments ago they touched moss-slick stone) while the light about them deepens. And then the Duke forces the seal that holds the thing closed, a seal never meant to be disturbed.

There is breaking, a parting along the wood seams.

As he does this, the Duke exhales a shuddering sigh, no longer conscious of her who stands a few feet away. Unaware of anything extraneous, he raises the lid with both hands and looks inside, into the gaping maw. . . .

But again she intrudes upon him. "Take the bones and dust, and arrange them. On the table surface, yes, and form them according to—"

"I know," he says. "Be silent."

And for once, possibly feeling the force blooming from him, she does not speak another word, only stands somehow immobilized, chilled, for her own vaguely private reasons, and looks on.

It must be noted at this point that there is no blood-letting to be involved. The Duke is impressed that she does not inquire after it, does not insist upon blood sacrifice. For it appears that she indeed knows the advanced details, the true techniques of profound-level arcane arts. Blood sorcery is not only of the dark, but it is also of the lower echelon of methodologies; a resurrection attempted via the killing of a living creature—a parasitic borrowing of the life force—will only result in a temporary animated golem, a zombie, a distasteful animatron without true autonomy or life, only to be directed by external forces.

But of course, since the act of resurrection has never been achieved by an ordinary mortal man, everything that follows is within the realm of theoretical.

The Duke begins to work. His hands are glowing like day lilies. There is something absolutely vibrant in the feel of him, an odd sensual vigor brewing and ready to explode forth.

Janerizel watches his gaunt form suddenly humming with active force, his sallow cheekbones prominent in a face filled with previously dormant but now extravagant beauty. His hair, with its tendrils of succulent honey-hue emphasized by candlelight, is no longer dulled by the night but now shimmers in a halo. There is a paradox of light and shadow about him, for the light comes from three sources, the two candles and *himself*.

His eyes are averted, looking intently down at the objects before him; it is a good thing too, not to see the eyes now. They are full of such things of sorcery that it's best not to witness unless one's own self is attuned to that same etheric sphere.

And so, not knowing what he perceives, she waits.

First, after moving the candles even farther to the opposite ends of the table, one on each side for a balance of illumination, he removes a skull from the box—the first puzzle piece. The skull's pearl surface is smooth, unmarred by corruption, and the bone itself does not appear to be polished with age. He lays it at the edge of the table upon the soft chamois cloth.

Several other larger bones follow. He seems to know intuitively where to place them—or maybe he has spent hours staring at anatomical drawings, though she doubts he's had experience with real cadavers—as he assembles a skeleton. The ribcage forms like the bowed wood of a rowing ship. She notes how odd it is that the bones seem to attach to each other readily, to lie in just the precise locations where they are placed and where they should be without collapsing, never falling apart after he rests them down, as though held by invisible tendons.

The bone structure on the table begins to take on a pulsing energy of its own. He works silently, his beautiful hands moving in a parody of a holy ritual, never missing the tiniest bone. Finally, when all that is left in the funeral box is dust, he turns it over, emptying the dust into one open palm (where it appears to dance and seethe for an instant, like living yeast).

And then, with a soundless cry of parted lips, he scatters it over the complete skeleton. The dust, in a cloud of fire-sparks, takes on slow motion. Billowing in the way of swirling snow, it floats gently down to settle over the bones.

Everything wavers then, and in a ghostly blur an image of a body begins to appear about the skeleton, then solidify. Rossian outstretches his fingers, stroking the outlines of the translucent flesh in an echo of sexual ecstasy, though his face as always shows no emotion; ecstasy is expressed through motion and touch.

A sudden squall of mist-laden wind; he pulls water out of the air, draws it in, and the mists coalesce and come to him. All around, the rock walls are stripped of their water slickness as he absorbs it, takes it into himself and directs it to the forming flesh. Flesh is water. . . .

Suddenly he is feeling dry, desiccated. . . . Around him the funnel of cold night wind is a parched breath of winter desert.

As the waters are absorbed, energy continues to flow from an arcane fountainhead contained in him. Janerizel can likely perceive with her own ethereal sense the tiny living cells forming out of the energy and the moisture drawn from the night air, beginning to multiply with unnatural speed. The matter, layers upon layers of gradual thickening, becomes solid completely, no longer semi-transparent, no longer showing through itself, through vaporous gossamer, the cloth surface of the table.

The body, complete at last, is female. It is however still pulsing with material instability, hairless, not quite alive and more akin to wax. She is beautifully unreal, this woman. And the

Duchess of White watches her emergence from out of nothing with an intense facial expression that can be understood as an incomprehensible mixture of affection, jealousy and some deeper emotions which are coming to the surface after being repressed for quite some time.

She appears to be jealous of this empty thing possessing the touch of his hands. . . . For, his elegant fingers are still moving against the now-resilient flesh, with every stoke bringing more natural color to the skin, delicious peach, a coral glow suddenly rising on the marble lips, and the scalp pierced by the light down of beginning hair. It is embryonic at first, yet quickly matures into a real deep auburn mane; it erupts like a forest, in waves, coming down her pale neck, bursting elsewhere on her body, eyelashes, skin-covering down. . . .

Or maybe the Duchess is jealous instead of his hands possessing the joy of this wondrous thing they are sculpting, and she craves to reach out and know the resiliency of the female for herself, know the smooth surface and the potential warmth underneath.

No matter; the woman lies unbreathing. Her lovely small breasts do not rise and fall under the expansion and contraction of the diaphragm; there is no air escaping her nostrils. And there is no pulse in her throat, no beating in her chest. A wax doll indeed.

He exclaims in frustration and stands back, his touch leaving the mannequin body. "I cannot!" he cries. "There's a certain level that I can't seem to reach—and thus she's not complete."

"You must," says Izelle; somehow she is imploring with her gaze. "For it is the same level you must attain in order to understand the force that binds you here in the castle. It's quite likely that long ago, the Just King only meant for each of us to know our own secret. This might be absurd, but I believe that all the secret powers of the Dukes are fundamentally the same. And they resonate on a single sorcerous level. It's the exact intensity and sphere of it, on which depends our freedom."

"Look at her," Rossian says meanwhile, the attention of his eyes never leaving the body before him. "She lies incomplete, yet—yet I can almost perceive what I seek, what I'm missing. So infinitely close to my understanding, yet a hair-breadth away."

Suddenly he turns to Janerizel. "Lady," he says, looking at her. "As you see, I've done this. I've conquered and indeed utilized my primeval distaste. Verily, I've converted death—or rather, the *nonbeing*—through my aversion, into its opposite, *existence*. Yet why can't I do more? I thought my knowledge of the arts was advanced indeed. Her body is almost alive, but not completely so. It exists, yes, but it does not *live*."

The state of being in existence, and life, he thinks in tumult, *are so close . . . so close. And yet they stand in two different spheres.*

It is odd what Izelle must feel then, seeing the expression of his eyes accompanying the words, for it is *trusting* and innocent, washed clean of sarcasm and replete with longing, the search for that which he cannot attain. He has been transfigured by his arcane act of making, made receptive, sensitive. And he is asking her, honestly asking without arrogance.

"I am not sure . . ." she says quietly, set back by this novelty, even though she knows and is sure. "There are the greater details that must be dispatched, specific things. For example, start her heart beating, the organs functioning. You were so particular to the tiny particles of being, the dust of life that comprises the cells of our flesh, that you never concerned yourself with the *movement*, the living general kinesis of her."

"Yes!" he exclaims. "What an imbecile, to overlook! Thank you for reminding me. Movement, yes! It's inherent in the living mechanism. I see you're aware of profound levels in your craft, yet—how do you know this? Unless—"

Izelle shrugs. "No, it's not quite what you infer. My secret is closely related to yours. Unfortunately it is not identical."

But again he is no longer listening, having approached his creation, and his hands begin their phosphorescent life-giving movement.

A shudder, light and half-real, moves through the form of the woman. The drum of life, the heart, is the epicenter of that shudder; suddenly, it happens. The drum starts its pounding automation. . . .

Blood rushes. Blood is blue and crimson and anemic-pale and dark with the riches of surrounding night, for it has been coalesced from the waters present in the night air; it is chilled by the cold and warmed by the passion of the one who sets it into pumping motion—and it is all one thing. Blood is moving, and thus, it is alive. The subterranean streams of it begin their sluggish activity in the veins and arteries, and continue to the tiniest passages of capillaries.

Her cheeks—the cheeks of the female creature—attain true subdermal coloration as a result. It's not merely the presence of blood under the skin, but of a moving, *seething* stream.

Her lungs quiver once, initially. Then, in a sharp intake they fill with air for the first time, billow, unfurl like sails, supported by the pressure of the diaphragm, while the body on the table convulses and falls back. Rossian's fingertips linger over her lips and nostrils to feel that air escaping and once more drawn in by the whirlpool of turbulence inside.

"She . . . lives?" whispers Izelle.

Rossian is silent, watching the body.

"My Lord? She—"

"*No.*" His voice is harsh. "No, she does not! Her body lives. Not *she*. Where is *she*?"

Where, where, where, where. . . .

"Only you would know the answer."

Agonized, he begins to pace, his face now twitching with frustrated emotion. Nerves pull at his eyelids, a vein throbs in his forehead, echoes in his throat.

It is unbearable.

"What?!" he cries. "What is the missing element?"

Izelle averts her eyes. "I think I begin to understand," she says quietly.

"*What*? Understand what, damn you?" Like a madman he turns on her.

But unperturbed, she continues in the same tone, staring off into the darkness of the night about them. "It's the *responsibility*. Yes, I remember now. When I was also faced with that—final moment, the *decision*, I too, balked unconsciously at the sudden realization of the magnitude of it all, the responsibility for another being. I knew then that I had the terrible ultimate control over the *act* of my power and the repercussions that would follow."

He watches her with agonized eyes.

"My Lord, can you at this moment imagine, understand what this all means? What it means for that body over there, that *thing*, to suddenly become a living self-aware being? Can you conceive of this Nairis—whoever she once was—getting up, smiling at you, and walking away of her own free will? For, somewhere in the ethereal sphere, her captive will cleaves to yours even now, and you must be the one to break with it in order to set her free. Can your pride and will endure such a parting?"

The Duke looks on, his eyes glittering with moisture in the candlelight. And *something* happens to him then, something in the intimate night. But it is not what she thinks.

It is his perception of her, the Duchess of White. All her former insignificance is suddenly effaced, transformed into forbidding will. He *sees* her then, sees *that* in her eyes, which he had only glimpsed briefly when holding her wrist-to-wrist, hearing the clockwork of her heartbeat and the impossibly dark gaping maw in her skull that terrified him. He knows what it is that makes her far more powerful than him with all his arcane learning and intensity, all his pent-up desire for freedom and his suppressed life force.

This doll with a rosebud mouth has attained the knowledge of her full power, while he has not.

She is potential force, curbed violent energy. She is an abyss of spheres, a universe without end. For, she knows how to pull from it, from the fabric of it all. . . .

And he does not.

. . . Not yet.

And yet—yes. It's the will and the responsibility, he knows and realizes he's known always.

And thus Duke Rossian approaches the corpse and for the last time forces his fear and awe of the death before him to lie in the open, in the forefront of his mind in a thin oil-slick coating of vulnerability. And for the first time, he allows himself to touch that fear—not a deep-set beast within him, but a shimmering illusion, a parasitic flimsy membrane. Fear reveals itself; it is a bubble to be popped. And then there's nothing on the other side, nothing but his self. He allows the *wanting* and the urge to take over, and he reaches for the responsibility.

He feels a rift.

He is cracked and patched together.

Responsibility flies to him like a falcon, his falcon, trained to return. Responsibility is merely the undeniability of certain things, the acceptance of reality for itself and not himself.

And in a pale smoky film, *something* comes away from his mind. His consciousness is now a sphere of new, strangely sharp *clarity*, as though a bubble of self has expanded to twice its size. The walls of his castle spin around him, rushing upwards, as he experiences vertigo and a grounding in the present moment—sharp awareness of the night's cold, the slight movement of air upon the numb skin of his face; gold flickering of two candles; the fuzzy microscopic chamois cloth surface; her body; body lying nude and perfect with the pump of lungs; two moths flying over the flames; overhead, sky, sky, sky. . . .

In his fixed grandeur of clarity, Rossian suddenly knows the exact meaning and result of any and all of his possible actions for that moment and all others to come—terrible, sharp, clean, perfect. And knowing, he realizes certain absolute inevitabilities and consequences. There are necessities of things arising as a result of other things. It is frightening, the unfurling of a new mindset.

Izelle never sees his eyes in that moment, is never later to be sure what it is that happens, but the candlelight knows.

It touches the gaunt man's face, caresses it once and flees, as he, inhuman, turns away while appearing to glance into the night.

The Duke stands before the wax-like body. There is absolute determination in his fluid movement, and this time he is sure.

His hands flare with light and he runs them down the living-dead flesh. Izelle can surely feel it, the fierce light, and her own hair stands on end all over her body, in sympathetic resonance and something *else*.

It is like a string being tuned. Power comes to a snap all around and resettles into a new harmonic key. The walls of the castle sing. The meta-sound surrounds Izelle, perfect as the pitch within her own self. And then there is a *rush* of something.

The woman lying on the table shudders, full-body, and opens her eyes. In the dim candlelight they are colorless spots of shadow, the irises only slightly paler than the dilated pupils.

Rossian, the light of his hands extinguished, shudders also, his vigor spent. He lurches forward powerfully against the table, across the body of her who is now truly *present* among them.

Everything afterwards is anticlimactic. Izelle gives a small scream, then quickly stifles it. She comes forward to help him, and now it seems she is unable to hold her tongue. The jester is allowed to surface; it is the mad aspect of herself. "Come, my Duke, it cannot be so bad now, that you faint away. You've brought her to life, yet you would as soon kill her again by the weight of your body falling on her delicate newborn frame."

Yet the nature of her touch to help him up belies the flippant words. Her small thin hand rests upon his arm with the faintest pressure of contact through velvet sleeve, as though she fears to hurt him. He has become a delicate bubble that can be broken with the point of a hair.

But he is himself again. He jerks away from her as though her fingers burn. "Don't—" he says weakly, but with the same obstinate dignity, and turns his full attention to the female lying before them, beautiful, nude, and alive.

Only, Nairis—whoever she once was, let her now be called thus—is obviously in shock. Her peculiar child-eyes stare in an infantile look of incomprehension; now that the Duke peers closer, leaning over her, they are blue as cornflowers. She is, he assumes, not an idiot, but apparently whatever she experiences now is so far from the usual manner of "birth" that it is impossible for her mind to grasp. He hopes the effect is temporary, or at best, if ancient memories do not come to her, she can learn quickly in order to assume a life in the here and now.

What has been done?

"I think you should call your servants, my Lord," the Duchess of White says softly. There is a weird expression in her eyes and she never looks at the newborn woman-child. "And get something to cover her with. Unless, that is—" And again, some perverse demon in her waxes profane—"Unless you are so bewitched by the display of *new* female flesh that you are unable to part from her."

Rossian, leaning close over Nairis, is indeed bewitched. His thoughts are different, his outlook modified, his senses scream. . . . Yet he is not about to reveal the difference. His voice is cold and profoundly normal, as he calls Harmion and gives instructions to the servants.

"She must be treated as a new-born child," he says gently, regarding Nairis, to Izelle. "It's as if I've engendered her. Although a woman in body, she is so innocent, her consciousness a blank. Strange how young she was when she died. Though, such youthful death could have been caused by childbirth or a simple pestilence. Her age holds no more than two decades, I would say—for I'm certain she is returned to us at the exact age of her death, as though time has been paused for her, and then, in a skip of centuries, it now resumes. What mysteries surround this death, I wonder? For that matter, what kind of antique time did she experience in her brief life, ages ago? But—whatever her past, it is no longer. One day I might question her when she is deemed to be strong enough. Meanwhile she must be looked after carefully. Too quickly exposed to life, her mind might come unbalanced. And then—"

"And then you would have one insane but beautiful Nairis on your hands," Izelle snaps. She is getting more and more irritated for a reason known only to herself. "Such a relationship just might promise pleasures, isn't it true, my Duke? Idyllic sensual pleasures for a man—*are* you the man I am supposing you to be?"

He straightens abruptly, his form still and inscrutable. "What? What in Heaven? You, my Lady, suggest things that are offensive."

But then, it's as if he is deflated, wrung out, and the cold energy of anger leaves his eyes, leaves him with the hollow place just below his lungs, and apathy. Now he deliberately ignores the Duchess, that little gadfly with a foul sting, and stands leaning over his creature Nairis—for yes, she has become his, hasn't she?

There is a never-before-seen kindness in his eyes. Inside, he feels a warm slow blooming of joy, a strange after-effect of creation. This is what the Deity must feel when the Deity creates the Universe; the scale is different yet the parallel remains.

The Duke then reaches out gently (his hands are trembling) to help the "new-born" one to sit up. His strong, expert fingers have lost their ruthless aplomb and are suddenly hesitating, for he is unsure where it is appropriate to touch her. And so he places them lightly underneath her shoulders, fingertips to skin which is feeling cool to the touch, for the night has its effect upon the living exposed flesh. He presses his fingers; they dig into her shoulders, soft, resilient; he lifts her up into a sitting position.

The creature Nairis obeys the directed pressure of his hands automatically, making small animal-infant sounds as she exhales, and her skin is covered with goose bumps from the compounded moments of chill. He tries not to look now, but her small plump breasts slide down her delicate ribcage while their roundness becomes pronounced on their underside; at the same time they are suddenly sharp-pointed.

The Duke looks away, then learns how to look without looking, to see her with his peripheral vision in order not to see lower, the smooth slender stomach, the oval depression of the navel, and continuing below—no. Her glassy eyes remain wide open, and he focuses there, so that it is easier to think of her as still unreal, an animated doll.

For, in those moments now that he is fully aware of this incarnate responsibility before him, the Duke is cold with terror and with the choices piling up, the temptations that are presented. And in thought he continues to blaspheme, as notions race past him, *Does a creator feel lust for his own creation, does Deity desire what is most innocent and unadulterated in the first instant of engendering, just before mortal corruption takes over?*

Izelle watches him. If she suspects what goes through him at that point, she is never to be sure. It is easier, instead, to let him be, and simply feel pity.

In that moment, Harmion, somehow knowing exactly what is required of him, returns to the open-sky chamber with maid-servants, with additional candles, and with a strange fixed look in his eyes. One maid brings with her a freshly laundered sheet to wrap about the nude woman-child. Their intrusion into this place of ritual is somehow peculiar and breaks the concentrated tension; the sheet is unfolded and its sharp revitalizing scent of lavender soap wafts on the cold air. Another maid brings soft fabric slippers, and a stack of additional linen.

The Duke stands back, torn out of a personal reverie, and allows the nude innocent to be concealed from his view and from the night by the generous sheet.

Nairis accepts the covering and shivers, her posture slumping as she withdraws into the sheet and herself. They gather around her and ever-so-gently, with the help of many hands, they teach the body of Nairis to get up.

She stands. Lovely and limber, yet she totters on her feet newly-shod in the satin slippers. She has to be led away, helped along like a rag doll. As she turns her back, her hair is glorious, a brown and red illusion of flow, nearly to her waist, shimmering in the candlelight. . . .

Izelle is watching, oddly frozen, unmoved by the sight. Impossibly, she is allowing them to take the woman-child away. It's as if some new emotion is tearing the Duchess in twain, so that it's easier simply to do nothing.

"Where should she be taken, M'Lord?" says Harmion, clearing his throat, pausing just barely at the doorway. And then he adds, "I recommend the Mad Queens Tower, if it's all the same with Your Grace. The quarters there are sufficiently presentable and ready for accommodation."

The Duke stares at him uncomprehending, it seems. Then, he comes to himself. "What? Oh . . . yes, that will be fine, Harmion. Please take her there. Help her . . . ready for the night."

When all are gone, all but the candle-lit table, the empty former box of death, and looming night-shadows, Rossian remains standing, immobilized, watching the night. His gaze slithers along the walls, averted from Izelle, and he takes deep breaths of the cold air.

"I am . . . sorry," she says. "I've implied things that are unworthy."

He remains as he is, never turning her way.

"Rossian? My Lord Duke?"

"You, my dear, have a malicious bent. Yes, I see it now. You called me *truly cruel,* but what do you call *yourself?*" He speaks unexpectedly in a hard voice, stronger than she imagines him to be capable of, and she is startled.

And then he turns, and she sees the truth—receptive wounded eyes, gleaming dark with moisture.

"Do you really think I am—like *that?*" he asks, and his voice fluctuates; is cracking. "That I would think of her with such filth? Her, whom I perceive only as a dear thing I have somehow *wrought?* To desire such sacrilege?"

Desiring sacrilege. Being profane. Do you really think that I—Mad inconclusive thought fragments begin to race in him, driven by fever. . . .

"I am sorry," she says again. "Forgive me, for I am indeed quite offensive, often intentionally, but sometimes not. Only—there is something about you, Lord, that touches me peculiarly—" She cuts off abruptly. Then, just as abruptly, she changes the subject. As she speaks, her voice rings bright, sending echoes against stone.

"Well, now that you presumably know your secret, would you care to test the castle boundary once more?"

Could it be that everything stills then, is suspended. The night air pauses in its flow. The stars stop their infinitesimal journey across the tiny patch of boundlessness overhead.

The Duchess holds her breath, watching him with unflinching eyes.

But the hurt-transfigured gaze of the Duke remains grim, and there is no new hopeful resolve in his voice, only weariness. "No," he says. "Not now—tomorrow. As I am now, I have no more strength for acts of power. . . ." And he throws back his head and glances with a shudder at the open sky overhead.

The Duchess of White averts her eyes, allowing him the privacy of weakness. He has earned it in full, tonight.

ଓଙ IV ଛଓଛ

A Dream of Falling

It is three past midnight. The Mad Queens Tower stands on the northernmost end of the castle grounds, as thick and squat a cylinder as any, one of the many rounded turrets that protrude in ancient tumescence from the baseline of the castle foundation.

The top of the tower does not narrow into a point. Rather, it has a flat roof which serves as an observation point, with thick crenellated parapets rising in a brim of protection. Wind hums through the crenels between the merlons and disappears into the gaping absolute darkness of the descending stairwell, in a twister, a whirlpool of aerial force. There it races down, down, down, falling without end, like a nightmare-dream.

Until it hits bottom, full force.

If wind were a man, it might be expected to die, as such things be told in the proverbial way of things.

They say, always wake up before you hit bottom.

Only, the bottom is no end, and the end is not the bottom. The base of the stairwell opens like a curling snake into a courtyard area, and here the wind and the clamoring air currents have the chance to continue their mad rush, onward and out into the world. The sky of the world is wrought of only a few degrees lesser darkness than the interior of the stairwell and other places hidden by stone walls, on account of a sprinkling of stars that lend a diffused glow to the heavens—throw a spoon of milk into a cauldron of pitch, stir to smoothness, and the dark remains, yet its nature has been altered just a degree beyond overt perception.

On such a night as this, with no moon, it is said that in the ancient days the noblewomen who reside in the tower would receive lovers. If the lover does not come, the high-born woman walks out onto the roof and waits for him, sometimes with a single flickering candle to signify her presence; its light can be seen for miles, a cry in the void. She waits, standing in the chill air of many nights, and eventually she becomes unbalanced. So many blue blood females wither with longing, with neglect or betrayal, with unrequited or simply forgotten love, that the tower, burdened with history, bears their woeful name.

Queens, Princesses, Duchesses, Countesses and lesser Ladies of various rank—wives and maidens, daughters and sisters—all are equal in the eyes of anguish, all are royalty of unfulfilled desire. In the moment of their emotional nadir they are all Mad Queens, tearing out their hair and gouging eyeballs, screaming and foaming, if only within the recesses of their broken minds. Meanwhile, their outsides often remain composed and placid till the end, numb hollow shells over roiling death inside.

The tower stands, has stood for decades unto centuries

unto stretches of time unaccounted, for the Dukedom of Violet is one of the oldest in the realm, and this place, the castle grounds, is older yet. There is a bit of irony that most recently the Mad Queens Tower houses neither Queens nor madwomen, nor any other tormented souls, but occasional guests of the living Duke.

Such as tonight.

The Duchess of White and the strange creature Nairis are both given elegant accommodations in the tower—as elegant as the crumbling castle permits. While the Duchess enjoys the services of a maid for the night, a change of clothing, a warm fire in the hearth, much perfumed linen and warm coverlets, a sleeping cap and gown of the softest fabric, a tray of sweet pastries and a hot tea service, Nairis—not much more cognizant than a newborn—is unveiled by three maids no less, dressed in a sleeping gown, placed on the chamberpot to no effect then finally success, cleaned up, spoon-fed a hot soup, scrubbed around the neck, face and ears, hair brushed till it crackles and gleams, and finally laid upon a feather bed upon which the slender body of Nairis sinks.

Nairis lies thus, listening with the precise awareness of a wild animal to each snapping twig and hissing spark of the fireplace, to each rustle and creak of settling stone (for even after all these centuries, the castle moves, breathing like an ancient legendary wyrm). She is warmed by a thick quilted coverlet and a hot brick wrapped in several layers of cotton. One maid has gone but two maids still hover over her even now, watching her motionless form, her gently flickering eyelids as they become groggy with the need for sleep.

But apparently, as many newborns, Nairis has the curious inability to fall asleep even when exhausted. And thus they come to rock her; one older buxom maid draws Nairis up to her motherly chest and moves to and fro, making soothing hum-

noises of a lullaby, while the very young one runs her fingers kindly over the forehead and tender filaments of auburn hair.

It must be noted that the buxom maid has been selected for this task because she is a nursing mother with a steady and reliable supply of milk. Before coming to attend Nairis she is told of the possibility that the strange young woman—who is explained to be suffering from a malady and is unable to understand or look after herself—might require a breast to suckle, just as a newborn, in which case the maid is ready to accommodate her.

Eventually all three become drowsy. Nairis is soothed and lies back against the feather bed, is covered and cosseted, and her eyes, overcast with languor, are finally closed.

Since she appears to be asleep, the two maids pull the draperies nearly closed around the great bed leaving just a small space to observe her, then make themselves comfortable in two large upholstered chairs. They have been told to stay with her overnight, to watch for any peculiarities, to handle any of her needs. And so they do as they are told for the most part, watching with one eye, as the common saying goes. The older maid is already snoring softly, chin sunken down toward the deep shadowed space between two fat bulging breasts, while the younger maid goes to bank the flames in the fireplace, stirs the coals, then clambers up into the other chair, feet curled up underneath her apron for extra warmth.

A single tallow candle remains lit on the side table.

By three o'clock past midnight, the candle is nearly down to one third of its column, with the rest of it pooling in the dish.

It is then the door of the chamber opens and a gaunt tall man enters the room.

The Duke makes no sound as he steps inside. It's an

uncanny ability that he has attained as a side-effect of his arcane learning—he can move in absolute silence and, if he desires, can make himself dissolve into abstract non-presence with nothing more than a subtle shift of focus. He employs this craft upon occasion to test himself, by passing within inches of oblivious servants in the hallways and listening to private conversations.

And now he uses his ability to stand and observe and then approach. He moves toward the bed and is undetected by the maids. The younger whimpers like a pup in her sleep and shifts her cramped position in the chair in restless slumber, while the older breathes heavily in a deep rumble; her bonnet has shifted slightly to expose wisps of corn-yellow hair.

The Duke moves past them both and draws part of the bed curtain aside so that the waning candle casts a clean radius of illumination over the sleeping Nairis. She is lying on her back, one slender arm thrown up on the pillow, coverlets bunched to one side exposing the shape of her waist and hips covered by the linen nightgown. Her long hair fans out along the pillow and coverlet, meanders in curling tendrils along the neckline of the gown and her chest, and obscures half her face in a natural tangle. The portions of her face that show are defined by clean lines, a slender angled chin that continues into an elegant neck, a delicate pulse at the throat.

He watches that pulse, mesmerized. What has drawn him here, but this? The pulse of her life flickering in and out of being, her rhythmic movement of lungs that he *hears* several floors away in a remote different tower as though they are grand bellows of a smithy, working in his mind.

He considers, *Does the Deity feel this urge toward the Creation, this pull to be with the offspring and observe?*

Indeed, is there a pang of terror that comes to grip his own lungs in a fist, fear that the creature left to fend for itself cannot be thus, cannot exist in stand-alone condition without the parent, maker, progenitor?

Or is he merely insane within his permanent condition of solitude? Is his reaction akin to that of a natural parent watching his newborn child, but he does not know it is thus?

Rossian looks at her and thinks, *No. It is not the same thing at all.* And he does not feel fatherly in the least, nor divine . . .

He feels profane.

The Duke knows of the function of sex, and is familiar with the cycle of procreation and the mechanics of the act involved for the human animal. Yet he never engages in such intimacy, for there is no one and nothing that can overcome the defenses of his inner reserve. Not even the internal urges of his body, the pulsing alchemical humours that course through his blood with regularity and bring him erotic dreams and nightly swellings of his genitals, not even this chronic restless longing for unknown release has sufficient influence over his aloof state.

Maybe it's that the Duke knows so well how to curtail one kind of longing—that for freedom—and as a result finds it easier to rule himself in all other things. Or maybe yet again, this is but a side effect of his proficiency in the arcane arts.

Whatever the reason, the Duke is virgin in body; in his mind he has allowed himself the full range of debauchery known to the imagination, and it seems to be enough to sustain him.

Until now.

The Duke watches Nairis, the living one, and thinks how she is thus because of him. Only hours ago, she is *not*—she is nothing, death, a bit of dust and desiccated bones. And now she moves; he has bestowed upon her automation, existence, life.

He is god to her mortality, the maker to her flesh.

And he feels a profound need to reach out and despoil

what he has brought into being. Far from being the sculptor of legend who creates a statue of a beauty, falls in love with her, and in the course of love brings marble to life, no—he is an artist locked in his studio with an intricate finished canvas over which he suddenly pours random globs of pigments in an elemental burst of creation-fury.

The maids continue sleeping and the candle burns lower still, while the Duke stands in atrophy of the senses and movement, watching the living canvas before him as she slumbers, innocent. She is his, this creature. So easy to take a fistful of that soft hair, and pull. . . . To maul her slender arms. To rip the linen cloth from her and see her center, her solar plexus, and what lies below.

And the Duke leans down and reaches out with his hand to run his fingers like a whisper upon the inside of her upturned arm. He feels a cool place on her skin, followed by a sudden warming, and, as his fingers continue slithering toward more tepid places, a deep heat—in sleep her living body burns.

And his own body responds, so that suddenly he is burning too, as though dreaming in sensual pleasure. He leans over Nairis, and feels himself growing, as his penis fills with the blood-humour and hardens, prodding at the confines of his clothing.

The maid stops her rhythmic snoring and coughs, without waking up; he glances her way to make sure, notes the rolling of her breasts engorged with milk as they pool sideways in her bodice while she lies draped against the padded armrests of the chair. The peculiarity of this arrangement affects him—the fact that all these other women are in the room, no matter how oblivious—and he feels an unexpected additional pang of desire; desire is misdirected and he has no conscious way of curbing it in this odd *moment* in particular.

The Duke responds by lifting up the lower folds of the nightgown that covers Nairis and pulling it up slowly and soft as a feather over his creature's thighs. Nairis makes a small noise but does not wake up; she too is under the thrall of his sorcerous invisibility and non-presence.

Her thighs are smooth and warm—ah, they are scalding-hot with the sleep fires. He separates them wider, taking care to move ever-so-lightly, then places one palm against the inside of her thigh-flesh. Somewhere higher up, that deep cleft of her female privates remains concealed by the coverlet and the gown which is bunched up just over that place.

He pauses, then with trembling fingers works the stays of his trousers in the front, the pouch that holds his genitals. Long seconds stream by and pull into infinite strings while his fingers catch on fabric, on loops, on idiot ties. Then, he is free. . . .

The trunk of his penis has grown thick and hot. He hears, feels, smells himself—the pungent vigorous meat is pulsing with his own heart's clockwork, only now there is no illusion of ever-slowing machinery but instead a speeding up, a fierce, violent quickening.

Only a few steps away the younger maid moans in her chair, a high pitched girlish timbre, followed by a light sigh.

The Duke feels the intruding sigh resound in his genitals with a wash of sensual urgency; the echo slides over him, it seems—if sound has a tangible physical mass, then this one is a caress of buttery smoothness, so that he feels a corresponding moan building in the back of his throat. He needs to release it, needs to make the sound himself, thick and low, a grunt. Instead, he parts his lips into a silent O.

And then he takes hold of himself down there, hand rubbing the nether side of his sack, then advancing onto the trunk with its subdermal prominent vein, the grotesque limb of ugly-beautiful, a tree-root, a gnarled thing that drives him to fierceness.

Nairis lies before him, heated with sleep, her white thighs displayed, while he abstains from touching her and instead closes his hand around his thick circumference—it is so thick, his fingers barely meet—and starts the violent pulling movement back and forth along the penis. Within moments, drops of an unfamiliar liquid begin to gather at the blunt tip.

Previously he does this only in dreams. His control for the greater part of his life is impeccable, and this is the first time he allows himself to be consumed by the choral rhythm of other living beings around him—consumed by the polyphony that is life.

He watches his female creature as he pants in a silent orgy of self-consumption, exhaling more harshly, louder, with each hand-stroke, while he nears *something* of which he is unsure but which he somehow knows profoundly from the pleasure-haze of his erotic dreams.

The buxom maid gives a loud rasping snore, a coarse shocking scrape of sound which acts upon him in an unexpected way to elicit a response. And in that moment he groans and lets go, blanks out, while his penis becomes a shooting cannon beyond his control.

Buttermilk—or a liquid that he initially perceives as buttermilk, although he knows it is his semen—blasts out of him in white and thick pressure-bursts, and it strikes the bedding and the coverlet, and splatters upon the white thighs of Nairis.

His living canvas is stained, despoiled (with something else of his that is vigorous and alive, the irony is undeniable), while he makes one long final groan of release, and sinks onto his knees on the edge of the bed. He is broken, a marionette with strings that have lost all tension, sprawling in a tangled pile of wood pieces. The illusion of living movement is gone. And he is shuddering with a chill after-effect of an irrevocable fracture of control.

The sleepers remain miraculously unaware and nothing has changed, it seems. Only the candle takes that moment to sputter in the last of its tallow, and the golden light goes out. The chamber is consumed with darkness and suddenly the world is very cold.

⊰⊱ V ⊱⊰
Following A Nondescript Sunrise

Dawn is here, chill and crisp, and clouds coalesce in grey streaks of varying degrees of pallor over the castle. In the faint blooming of light the castle is but an arbitrary rock formation standing in silhouette against the transforming sky that holds in it a suggestion, a foreshadowing of the sun, while the cloud cover veils it, extending its cool respite in twilight.

Grey and silver is the light of intimacy. Such is the inviting sensation achieved at the rare moments when the world appears to have no color. There is something placid in the surface of a grey sea or the overhang of silver sky. When rain comes thick as a curtain, again, color is diffused and dissipated, and all that remains is the same as what's on the inside of one's eyelids.

This particular dawn is quite the epitome; its intimate huelessness calls all unto itself, into its pallid grey places, to come and be soothed in the infancy of light. . . .

Duke Rossian of Violet sleeps right through it. Unlike his usual self he sleeps past the faint earliest glimmer in the east as can be seen from the windows of the easternmost tower where he frequently stands waiting for the spectacle. He sleeps through the luminous ghost-sky and the deepening of incandescence as it takes the edges of heaven along the horizon, and night begins to melt away.

The Duke comes awake eventually and it is now a sun-lit morning. For a moment he is an innocent, his mind emerged from the *elsewhere* of sleep equal to the consciousness of a newborn.

And then he remembers. Remembers another such child mind. And the memory and all else that goes with it wrenches him with a pang of terror followed by a wave of sickness. He tries to think what is the meaning of abomination. And somehow, there is no longer an answer. Edges are blurred and old familiar definitions do not seem to fit but overlap, while descriptions collapse into senselessness of random detail.

The mind itself is out of focus. Kaleidoscopic patterns are now random shattered glass; ideas fall together in sham bits of sparkle treasure from a magpie's nest.

The Duke rises from his bed and examines his body. As he stands to void himself, holding the chamberpot in one hand and himself in the other, he watches the arc of his urine and thinks of what else comes out with a more rhythmic violence. His body is unblemished and healthy, and he is bursting with the life force.

Does he not prove it sufficiently, last night? If not, then what exactly does he prove? What has been done?

Mind continues to spin, a child's top that is incapable of stopping.

In addition to all the other clamor in his mind he also knows that now he will be expected to test the boundary of his castle. And imagining the ordeal ahead of him, he tarries, while a gnawing sickly fear commences working at his insides.

Whatever has been done, the world is changed in a plurality—his world. For when change comes, it comes on its own terms, and with a retinue.

At some point Harmion knocks politely on the bedchamber door, reminding His Grace not only of a cold breakfast, but of a certain annoyance called the Duchess of White waiting for him. No mention is made of Nairis, and indeed at the thought of *her* whatever is burrowing in his gut takes a deeper wrenching bite.

The Duke of Violet mutters as he quickly dresses himself without assistance, his actions punctuated by stabbing thoughts. *She is, she lives, I gave her life. . . .*

And then, *What will happen now? She is. She lives. At which point does she become mine or cease being mine?*

Every motion he makes, it seems she hovers nearby, Nairis.

Down a flight of narrow stairs he descends from his personal sleeping quarters, and Janerizel, the eccentric Duchess of White, stands waiting outside his study. She is dressed exactly as the previous day, in her self-mocking outfit.

He stops in sudden consternation, while color surges in his cheeks and as quickly recedes. For, now he is fading, and his cheeks are fading, and his breath has become faint as he watches her. There is no reason this should be happening, the Duke thinks. And yet, it does.

The Duchess looks at him with her great weird eyes. She is waiting for something. He hardly notices that her right hand carelessly twirls a rose blossom on a long stem, a cut procured from his castle's gardens. Instead, he is looking at her rosebud mouth.

She steps forward, cheerful in tone, but her expression remains strange. As a proper lady would, out of blue-blood habit, she offers her hand. "Good morning, my Lord Rossian."

He is not sure why, but his first reaction is to jerk away from her. Fortunately, his control (shattered so badly the night before, three o'clock past midnight) is now again at his disposal, and he is able to remain impassive and endure the proximity.

Why endure? What in the world makes me think this way, instead of—

In order to see what he is capable of in the here and now, the Duke touches her hand in elegant politeness, and doing so he cringes inside. Continuing to cringe, he takes her hand and holds it. Then, as deep-inbred etiquette demands, he raises it to his lips. The hallway seems to press down on him, stifling with permanent dusk, here where there are no windows to reveal the daylight. The outside of her hand is a cool shock against his lips.

"And to you, Lady. Good morning. My apologies for my tardiness out of bed this morning."

His words are smooth and faultless as ever they can be, and yet in a new peculiar way they are kind toward the Duchess, as though he has decided to forgo his rude sarcasm that he saves for his unwanted guests. Indeed, words seem overly easy, and he considers them as they issue forth. He listens to himself, listens for any indication of *change*.

She too appears to be remarkably understanding. "No apologies necessary. You were exhausted by yesterday's extraordinary efforts. It's well known that the arcane acts drain the spirit and the flesh immensely. In fact, you must partake of food as soon as possible to restore yourself for what lies ahead. Oh . . . and how is she, Nairis?"

The Duke is suddenly bloodless, cold, and can hardly feel his face. He is glad for the dusk of the hallway, and almost indifferent to the muted paucity of air, for it seems he no longer requires it—no longer requires to breathe.

"I expect she is unchanged since last night. She has been accommodated in quarters similar to yours, and cared for—more than adequately—by several of my servants. Indeed, there's no need to be concerned on her behalf anymore, for she may take a long time if ever to regain her memory and her former ancient self. . . ."

Words come out of him in a measured, punctuated stream, and he speaks so calmly that he is beatific, until the language peters out. Then, nothing remains but silence.

"Oh . . ." the Duchess says. "But—but I assumed that she—I mean, I expected that she might come along with us, with me, that is. . . . After all, one might say she's been placed into my care by the circumstances—"

"Or, one might say, the circumstances of her restoration, the miracle of life returned to her through my efforts, indicate that she has been placed under *my* care."

All veneer of politeness is effaced. The Duchess glares at him, and she is once again a banshee. "What, my Lord? *Your* care? After the sorry muddle you've made of her resurrection? Admit it, she has the wits of a sheep and less than the awareness of a suckling infant!"

The Duke is suddenly burning. Cold fury fills him so that he cannot breathe yet again, only now for another reason.

"You dare to belittle my effort?" he exclaims. "What have you done for her but carry her bones around my castle? And my Lady, you must indeed think me a simpleton, for you have told me a blatant lie about this creature that we both seem to claim. . . ."

He continues, "You are unaware that last night after I took my leave, I spent several long hours perusing the records of the royal houses of the realm, all genealogical lines of succession, going as far back as there is recorded history. And nowhere is there a mention of a Duchess or even a remote blue blood by the name of Nairis the Fabled One, or even just Nairis. She does not exist! I've found one mention of a Nairis who served as a companion to the third Duchess of Blue, but that ancient and long-dead female was no more than a servant of the chamber, and she died a crone in her ripe old age!"

The Duke pauses, and the expression of his eyes is feverish. "And so, you lie, my dear. Your motives are unclear, and all I can now surmise is that this deceased young woman whom I resurrected last night is someone who matters to you in particular, and maybe there is even more to this convoluted story. Would you, at last, care to elaborate? I must have the truth!"

The Duchess parts her rosebud mouth, her lips delicate and succulent, as she is about to rant or spin tales or further deceive. And then she shuts them and takes a deep breath.

"First, Your Grace's breakfast . . ." And with a slight inclination of her head and a mockery of a curtsy she motions the Duke into his study.

The next hour is a haze of necessity. The Duke breaks his fast quickly by gulping down something he cannot remember to taste from a warmed tray brought up to him by Harmion (at the same time taking odd care to abstain from meat, for suddenly he is incapable of eating dead flesh, which might be another after-effect of his act of power), while Izelle chatters flippantly about the weather and the weave of the tapestries and the tomes scattered over his work table and all about the room.

He knows he must eat, so he ignores everything until

nourishment is consumed and piles warmly inside him. He is amused at her insistence that he eat and at how she is unaware that in fact he does so the for the second time since their dinner last night—that at four past midnight he consumes food in the darkness after leaving a certain chamber in the Mad Queens Tower.

When the spirit and the flesh are drained, sustenance must be sought. Oh, how well he knows it.

He finishes breakfast and puts down the bone porcelain cup with the last of its contents in dregs on the bottom. It clinks delicately against the bowl, and sunlight swirls along its gilded rim.

Izelle chooses the moment to settle in a great chair across from him. Sunlight glares into the chamber from his favorite window and illuminates her grotesque cap and half of her face, emphasizing the doll-like prettiness, the rounded apples of her cheeks.

"I will no longer do you the dishonor of duplicity," the Duchess says.

"I am glad."

"Truth is a bit more complicated than I am prepared to divulge. Not because I am unwilling, but because I am unsure where to begin. . . ."

For the first time the Duke gives her an effortless smile. "Begin," he says, "with yourself."

Izelle sighs. "Very well. Know then, that I am not the Duchess of White—Nairis is."

He stares, unblinking.

Izelle removes her cap and drops it on top of an open volume. Underneath, her dark hair is ruffled and wild, and she is so much a doll whose wig has been pulled by some unruly little girl for all of her childhood.

"Nairis—well, she is not, I mean, it's not her true name—but she *is* my sister. And that vendor was in her service, of course—I had him carry her box into your castle. Nairis . . . For years we used to play at Princesses of the ancient land called Aegypt, and eventually we were both Queens, naturally. She was Nairis the Fabled One, and I was Volatris the Graceful One. Not that I've ever been graceful, on the contrary. Nairis—I mean, Izelle—she was the graceful one. She was also beautiful, wise, intelligent, kind, perfect as a crystal vase. Still is, as you know. And she was gloriously slender and tall, even when she was seven or eight, a year older than me. And I was just this short and fat and idiot child who laughed like a crow and ate too many pastries."

"What is your true name, then?" the Duke says softly.

"Cora," she replies. "No, wait, I am sorry . . . I did tell you, no more deceit. I always wished they'd called me Cora. Or even Clara. Or better yet, Clarissa, which sounds light as a feather. Instead they shackled me with Molly. Which is short for Mollyanne or maybe Meredith, or even Mary, or Marie. Only, in truth, I am unsure. Mother and father both died before I could ask, and the birth name is recorded in our chapel as Molly."

"Molly," he says, testing the sound.

"Yes, what a nasty name, isn't it?" she says. "Vulgar as myself."

"Not particularly original, but neither is it all that unsavory," he replies, watching her squirm. "So, you took your sister's name. How did that come about? Should I ask how she died? I do have some idea, so you needn't be afraid to speak freely."

Molly gets up from her chair, and he notices she is still holding the rose in one hand, while her cap lying on the table is forgotten. The blossom is a tea rose, deep bloody crimson, so dark that it is rich as velvet, and the perfume that comes from it is potent musk. The stem is thick and pale green and the thorns are sparse. She twirls it between her fingers.

"I'll tell you, yes. But if I may ask, my Lord, would you come downstairs with me, out into the open? The sun is bright there, and I must—I have something to show you."

He complies silently, this time without any protest. After winding down several flights of stairs, they come out into the courtyard.

The scorching sun shines down this great stone "well," while the gates of iron stand open.

The gates. . . . These are the gates to the world outside the castle.

There, the whole universe continues, outside and beyond. A sand road rolls in a carpet of yellow gold, and all about, a green brilliant countryside.

How many times, countless times, he stands here thus, feeling the breeze wash over his face, seeing that familiar nearest birch tree out next to the road, knowing that he would never feel its living white bark with his hands. . . .

Rossian squints in the sun, white-skinned and deathly, and unused to such exposure. Whatever virile color he possesses is suddenly rendered inadequate by the reality of daylight.

And yet, how marvelous he must appear to this Molly formerly known as Izelle, the wind whipping his honey hair into a golden frenzy, his eyes, when not squinting, revealing a multitude of violet and blue hues. There is the proud gauntness of his jaw, the fine immaculate cuff-lace of his shirt. He belongs here, in the bright open, under the dome of sky. . . .

Molly sniffs the lush flower that she holds, drawing it close to her face, so that her perky button nose is concealed in the velvet petals. "My Lord. . . ." She is about to speak something important, it seems.

Eyes still narrowed from the world's brightness, Rossian glances at her.

But Molly does not speak. She glances instead in the direction of the open gates and nods to him.

The Duke considers that the moment is at hand.

Ah. . . . In that instant it seems the wind is blowing their way in particular, past the invisible occult barrier, with such ease that it is once again on the verge of impossible to believe it's there. Rich air comes in a stream of clean force inside the gates, carrying with it scents of wildflowers and honeysuckle from the meadowlands, a fierce elixir of the outdoors.

The Duke inhales it, growing dizzy with the unfurling of his lungs, the heady pressure inside.

"So, my Lady . . . " he says, feeling the warmth of the sun against the skin of his face. "I suppose I must do it now. It's not to be postponed. Though, there is nothing worse than the overturning of one's final hope. And yet—might as well get the inevitable over with."

"Yes," she says softly. And then, "My Lord, before you continue—Rossian, wait. First, I need to show you something."

And for the first time Molly truly *looks* him in the eyes. There is a subtle difference between simply looking to examine, looking to address, and facing another with conviction. There are masterfully complex looks that present an intended effect, sideways looks designed to confuse or beguile, insidious and stealth glimpses that go unnoticed. Some looks are tangible projectiles, shots of intensity, quick, fierce, stabs in the heart. Other looks are bland, forthright, or nearly vacant for the lack of true engagement. And yet other looks are forceful, insisting, nigh physical touches of warmth, affection, concern.

Molly's look is a revelation. She lifts an invisible veil

and shows him her *self*—past the skin, past the tissue and bone and blood.

The Duke, who just about puts his foot forward to advance toward the gates, stops. He is mesmerized.

Despite the fresh pleasant breeze streaming at him, there is a shiver-inducing chill in the air—nay, in his mind—as he looks and *sees* her. "I remember . . ." he says breathlessly. "Did you not say your arcane secret is somehow related to mine?"

"Yes . . ." Molly barely responds. And at last he knows what is on the inside, what it is that lurks just beyond her tragic eyes.

"Look closely, my Lord . . ." she says. "Look."

At first he merely watches the bottomless abyss that opens in *her* eyes; he does not consciously attend what she means, or where to look beyond her centerpoint of face.

But soon the in-rush of power about them points directly to the correct spot; not her face, but below, no, lower yet. He feels it pulling, a hand of wind, drawing him to the invisible flow, an aerial funnel that moves beyond sight but takes his gaze down, lower, binds and drags him. . . .

Molly suddenly averts her eyes—they are filled with roiling sorcery—and he feels the line of contact between them breaking with a snap. But the invisible force-vortex continues pulling his attention, engaging his focus, and so he watches, of all things, the splendid tea rose blossom in her hand.

If this were nighttime, he might never notice. . . . But now, in the light of day, *darkness* comes in an eerie materialization of smoke, seeps into being from an *elsewhere* and begins to gather about Molly's fingers. As though a shadow of mottled sunlight through moving leaves of a tree is cast momentarily over her fingers, over the place she holds the flower stem. Yet—there is no tree nearby, nothing to cast a shadow. The castle bulwarks here loom in clean straight lines, devoid of crenellation at the edges, devoid of anything that might reduce the phenomenon to a natural explanation.

She stands (onlookers might assume she is but deep in thought), and ponders the flower before her, motionless, locked in the arcane *process* that is taking place.

In a cloud of dust, the darkness pouring from her hand permeates the air all about the blossom, and it begins to wilt, discoloring and then curling up into a dry husk, with the unnatural swiftness of sped-up time. Musky burgundy velvet is no longer; the rose petals curve then twist, invert upon themselves and dry preternaturally. Their deep redolent scent is gone, effaced into the ether.

Water departs, together with life.

Another heartbeat, and only grey dust fills Molly's small palm. It runs through her fingers, and is scattered by the vigorous wind. Darkness too is gone, fading into dappled sunlight, and in its place comes the homogeneity of clean day glare.

Molly stands, saying nothing, a vacant expression in her eyes. And then, in the culmination of divulged intimacy, she weeps.

The Duke finds the sunlight harsh, a cruel whitewashing glare, and he narrows his eyes even more, in an act of retreating.

"Oh. . . ." He exhales. "Lady. . . ."

"I'm death!" she cries, weeping louder now. There is something childish and horrible about her shaking frame. "*Now do you see . . . what I am? Abomination!*"

With a peculiar calm settling over him, pieces of information coalescing, he is drawn to move toward her, to console, and yet, he is held in place. There is a confusion of various different emotions, for now Rossian knows for certain that his original supposition is correct, and with this realization for the first time comes a kind of relief. At the same time a coincidental thought occurs to him; it is not *she* herself that he feels *aversion* for, but the nature of her power.

For some reason it pleases him. It pleases him not to feel aversion for *her*.

"Allow me to guess," he says. "The power of the Dukedom of White is in fact identical to mine. Your sister and you attempted something arcane and complicated to bypass the barrier of your castle, and the effort went awry. The backlash of the force exchange turned upon her, killing her, and simultaneously imbuing you with the inverse nature of her power."

Sobbing, Molly nods. "I killed her . . ." she chokes out, gasping between sobs. "Killed . . . my Nairis. We . . . we planned a temporary transfer of power . . . from her to me. Just for a moment! In the precise instant as it happened, she was supposed to cross—cross the barrier, and then she was to receive the force back into herself. It was to be a trick, a silly brilliant workaround to fool the castle . . . But . . . but when I channeled the power back into her, it was *wrong*, it was corrupted, life into death, and she turned black as coals and crumbled—before my eyes!—my beautiful tall sister screamed and turned charred and shrunken, and she burned, and there was only bones and ash and—"

Rending terrible sobs return, and Molly is shaking.

"You could not know this would happen," the Duke says kindly.

"But oh, we did! We thought of it, we even discussed the possibility! Izelle, the silly obstinate girl, oh, she laughed and told me to put her in a box in case she died, and to collect her ashes if she burned and make sure they were all in one place resting on pretty cloth, as they did in ancient Aegypt. . . . And now that very power, that horrible thing that killed her, is a part of my nature! It is in me forever, it sits inside, death, death, *her* death sits inside!"

Molly struggles for breath between harsh sobs; she screams, bends over forward and holds herself slowly as she begins to collapse. She is in a foetal bundle on the beaten earth and stone of the ground, contorting in agony underneath the bright sun.

Rossian finds himself completely frozen, realizing in self-horror that he is so incapable of responding to another's sudden pain on an emotional level that he cannot decide between his own emotions, cannot find it in himself to do anything. He feels the urge to say cruel things, "Don't be a gusher, my Lady . . . Stop your theatrics and compose your pitiful self." But thankfully he does not.

Instead he says, "Well, this at least explains in part our relationship. The frequent antagonism, conflict, the constant sense of being at odds with each other, grating on edge—"

"Relationship?" she cries, wiping tears and snot with the back of her hand. "You don't know the half of it! Do you think this is all? That I am all done with you?"

Shivering from a fever in the brilliant sun, she continues. "I came here, to you, Lord, so that you could bring my sister back! You, with your clean uncorrupted power, with its fountainhead reaching into the great common well of force, surely you could perform this feat, as natural as the act of breathing is to you—"

"Why me? What of the other Dukes?" he asks.

"Because"—Molly is raving; her face is once again a shriveled mess of tears—"Because the others are impotent idiots! The Duke of Yellow is a doddering drooling senile who never did anything in all of his life to discover the nature of his secret. He rots in his castle as did his father before him, and they will bury him in the vault—thankfully the line ends with him. The Duchess of Red is too busy amassing a fortune in trade and fine wines, too busy directing the planting of vineyards to even open a history codex! The Duke of Green is a weak-minded fop with artistic pretensions who likes to dress up in his wife's crinoline ball gowns and heels to put on masque performances before his circle of cronies. The Dukes of Black and Orange are dead with no heirs, and it turns out the regents are not bound by their castles. The Duchess of Blue and her twin brother are engaged in earnest study yet show no aptitude for the arcane arts, and are ineffectual."

She pauses with a gasp, staring up at him. "That leaves only you. Now do you see why?"

Whatever the Duke is about to retort is interrupted by the appearance of Harmion. As the wind continues to blow strongly through the gates, the butler emerges from the front entrance and hurries in their direction forgetting his usual dignified pace. He is followed by a skinny wisp of a maid who runs behind him, whimpering and wringing her hands.

"Your Grace, the Duke, my pardon! Your Grace!"

Rossian watches their approach.

"M'Lord, terrible, terrible news," Harmion exclaims, then stops short of breath, in a fit of coughing.

"Tis the young lady, m'Lord!" interjects the maid. "She be dead, m'Lord!"

"What?"

"We watch over her, an' she was sleeping all fine less'n a quarter hour ago, no more. But then, just now suddenly, she starts up, an' her eyes are all terrible, all big as saucers, m'Lord. An' then she falls back on the bed an' she turns all white'n blue, then all black an' she be dust and bones! Oh, an' m'Lord, earlier in the morning, Jennie an' I both dreamt of an incubus all night, an' when we wake, we sees his unholy seed spilled on her bedding, m'Lord! Oh, woe is us, there's a demon incubus in the castle! He killed 'er, surely he did!"

"What nonsense," the Duke replies softly, and his voice is rich with potential intensity. "Filthy superstition, girl. There's no such thing as demons. And what you call an incubus is but a figment of a dream, or a flesh and blood man disguised and welcomed in secret by a woman who needs a reason to deny the meeting. . . ."

"Well, one thing's a certainty. The so-called Nairis is dead, my Lord," says Harmion, wheezing, but recovered enough to speak at last. "I checked the bed myself, and there are only . . . pardon me . . . dry remains. Very peculiar and certainly terrifying, not even a body is left. And the girls here claim they watched the transformation happen—a living woman, my Lord. She fell apart before their eyes, only minutes ago from now."

"Thank you, Harmion," the Duke says. "I do believe you. Now, go and make sure that all is untouched in that unfortunate bedchamber. Do not allow anyone else to enter. I'll be there . . . shortly."

Harmion nods, used to the peculiarities of serving his master. He knows there are occult happenings, has observed evidence of such upon occasion, and is not particularly surprised even now—or at least not too much. And thus he sets out, back inside, with the maid walking behind him. The maid casts wide-eyed, frightened looks at her Lord the Duke, as though the words he tells are blasphemous enough to conjure an army of demon incubi now, just to prove him wrong and punish the whole lot of them.

When the two serving staff disappear, Molly speaks in a

stumbling voice, her eyes liquid with tears and brimming with deep anguish. "Why d-did you tell her that d-demons do not exist? You . . . know very well they do. You know what an infinite number of—of layers there is beyond this material fabric. You know the other arcane spheres—"

"Yes," he replies, grim. "I know indeed. But the ordinary uninitiated must not know. You understand yourself how such a thing must never be admitted. Why even ask me such a question?"

"Yes, but, but—"

"But what?"

In response Molly wails. She shudders and weeps as though she is a torrent, and it makes no sense until he realizes why she is weeping really. Or maybe he does not realize at all, dense and unfeeling and remote even then.

"Nairis . . ." he says. "So, then. My act of resurrection last night was for nothing. A temporary thing. Or maybe it's that she did not come fully into her own self, was incomplete, as we saw by her mental state? Only, I was so certain that life had taken a solid hold in her. . . . I wonder."

Molly sobs, wild and futile.

"No . . . it is *I*," she finally manages to say. "I killed her . . . *again!* The act of death, the withering of the rose flower I demonstrated to you in idiot disregard of possible causality, it was to blame! As the flower died, so did Nairis! I could sense it, I knew it was happening but did not want to admit, could not admit, ever, could not *stop*—"

"But—" the Duke says, "I don't see how you might have undone my intricate effort by a mere shriveling of a branch, and being so many feet away?"

"Oh, you must restore her again, my Lord! *Please*, I beg you!" Molly gasps out, ignoring his attempt at reasoning. "Only this time you must do it true, do it so that life can not be so easily defeated by corruption!"

Life is constantly defeated by corruption, he wants to say. *Though, somehow it persists. Maybe therein lies the key, in the surmounting of seemingly impossible odds?*

"I will do what I can," he says coldly. "But I must first try this thing, here, since we've come so far.

The Duke ignores her whimpering, her pitiful sounds, and walks suddenly toward the open gates.

Toward the barrier.

It seems that for a moment, something fleeting passes over the face of the sun. Brightness of day seems diminished, just for a split instant. Again, a shadow of dappled sunlight comes out of nowhere, but this time it seems to slither over all of the open sky, casting the courtyard into momentary gloom.

For the first time in his life, the Duke *feels* the barrier before he even touches it. It is a solid presence, a thing of metaphysical matter, of occult mass and solidity, yes. . . . And it stretches thick and vibrant on a different plane, one that is perceived only in a special compartment of his mind.

Rossian stops at the gates. He is washed by the wild impossible freshness of wind. He knows that if he is to move forward but an inch, his nose, his cheeks will touch *it*. But first, his tiny hairs on the skin will know. They will prickle, bristle, raise up bumps alongside his pores, stand on end, and there will be a charge of force in the air, a familiar buzzing in his face as he *touches*. . . .

Today there is something different about his awareness of the barrier. It's as if he knows exactly which intricate lever in the ethereal mechanism will raise it up and bring it down. He knows that he can reach out and push or pull something, grasp it just so, and the whole thing will collapse like a tall theatrical stage curtain.

The barrier, why, it is flimsy! A mere cobweb. . . .

His fingers curl and flex in anticipation, for he knows now he can move a single muscle and tear a ragged hole into some gaping *otherplace*. Ever since yesterday, when he pours and shapes life-force from himself and harvests it from the fabric of the world, then gathers it into one focused place, he knows how to do this thing.

Indeed, he suddenly has a terrifying thought—just as one pulls a stage drapery and suddenly a whole vista of a grand theater is revealed, he can pull and reveal endlessly the fabric that makes up the universe! And it will come falling, falling down on him in thick soft folds. . . . The air will fall first, and then the sky with its fixed lights, heaven toppling gently, and then, as he keeps pulling, the firmament underneath will begin buckling as though it were a carpet that he was grabbing at from under his own feet. . . .

He thinks this, and he somehow *knows* it to be true; he can do it. He can unravel the world just as he can make his way easily now, forward across the barrier, a knife cutting into butter. . . .

Power runs through him in a thousand ants crawling up and down his arms, his back, his face and every bit of surface of his skin.

The Duke puts his hand up and stretches his index finger forward and gently pushes.

There is a tingle, a painful crawling intensity, as always when he confronts the barrier. Only this time, he is touching past it and around it, as though he is wearing special protective gloves of force.

His finger moves forward and *through*.

His finger touches the air on the outside. Touches

freedom.

And in that instant as he makes the hole, he senses the delicate fragility of the barrier curtain. He senses how far it goes in all directions into infinity, and that what he's done by putting in a fingertip is already enough to collapse a mountain range . . . which will only be the beginning.

Sudden lore-fragments out of histories come to mind, codexes of strange notions that he knows rather well and casually, for he considers it to be foolery, for so long—the notion that the Just King contains and binds the forces of the Dukes not in order to punish but in order to preserve the verdant realm itself, to ground the power of life in the land. Other notions, of pooling waters, of holding them back—the Duke thinks, remembers—that the world is a garden because of this binding, that it must not be relinquished, must not be abandoned, else there will be a great flood—

It is the true nature of the secret.

And Duke Rossian of Violet is gripped in the intestines with the hand of immense terror at the knowledge; it is the tree of knowledge from that garden, for he has suddenly tasted the eye-opening fruit.

His fingertip buzzes in his mind if such a thing were possible—as it sits halfway through the barrier like a blunt needle, plugging the outside away from the inside, or the other way around.

Inside, outside, inside, outside. This side and that—interchangeable?

If he moves his finger forward, things will begin to collapse—all things. If he moves it back, inside, toward himself—who is to say the same thing might not happen anyway? The breach exists, and the barrier has been compromised.

The Duke slowly begins to withdraw his finger back inward, as he simultaneously reaches out with all the resources of his mind to pull the broken edges back together, quickly, desperately—to sew it shut, paste it, weave it, heal it, seal it—all imaginary visions of mending come into play.

For an infinite, interminable moment, *something* is happening.

At last the tingling is gone, and he senses the hole is no longer. How strong the mended place is, he does not know. But at least he knows that a certain collapse has been averted. . . .

"My Lord?" Molly speaks over and over, he comes to realize. She has been calling him for several moments now, but only now is he capable of hearing, or perceiving with his normal senses.

"What are you doing, Lord Rossian?"

He steps backward, putting several feet of safety between him and the temptation of the gates. And then he turns to her.

"Nothing. Let us go to attend your sister," he says in a dead voice.

And with these words the Duke turns back from the glory of the wind and sunlight and returns into his castle.

ೞଊ VI ଊଚ
Sacrifice

Nairis lies—or rather, her blackened remains lie—in a pile of soot on the white linen sheets of the bed. Bones and charred fragments are scattered in a shape that is vaguely human.

Standing over the bed, Rossian feels a wash of anger at the futility of it. He performs a miracle once (even now it makes his mind reel to think what he is capable of doing), and now he must recreate it. So different, now that the artist has his work destroyed by an outside force, so different a feeling, this anger; the presumption, the audacity of ultimate control has been taken from him, and it's what infuriates.

What makes me different from the Deity? he thinks in bitter rage. *I can call up life. And with a flick of the finger I can cast down all of creation. . . . What makes me different? Is it that someone else can come along and affect my living artwork?*

His thoughts continue a disjointed dance as he notices a faint, barely noticeable series of creamy stains along the coverlet in places where something has been splattered recently; he knows it for what it is, and feels a wash of cold memory—

No, stop. He must stop thinking in that direction, for it does not matter now.

I do what I will. Create, despoil, recreate at will, again and again. It is my prerogative.

Molly stands next to him, and she touches him on the shirtsleeve, so that inside him the life force recoils from her death. "Please . . ." she says. And her subsequent words seem to echo his thoughts, as though she reads his mind. "You must try to bring her back again. You're the greatest living master of the hidden arts. We both know that if there's anyone in all the world, then it's only you who can . . . do it. . . ."

"I'll wait until night," he muses to himself.

But she interrupts. "No," she says. "Now, please. Night is when the arcane forces are at their strongest, true. And yet, daytime, precise noon, is when the living force is at its height. And since what you attempt is the manipulation of the life force itself, the greatest of acts of power, it will work better, I think, if you begin now."

"Very well."

And suddenly he is raising his hands, running them inches above the charred remains, stroking the air just above. Cool luster comes from his hands, and it mixes with the bright daylight pouring in from the large window of this chamber. Gold warmth and pallor, the light blends with itself, while Molly makes a little sound and steps back. Now it is her death recoiling from the living forces being manipulated here.

The Duke works quickly. This time he knows exactly what is to be done; there is no hesitation as he reaches into the golden daylight-suffused air around him and pulls in elements of energy waveform, as though dipping his hands into containers of salt, flour, sugar powder, tangible particles that are everywhere, and so nearby as to be everpresent for one who knows *how* to look.

In moments, a familiar body's outline begins to take shape once again, at first translucent and delicate as though she is a mold poured from water. Shadow-forms that are internal organs can be seen, and the network of blood vessels branches out in fine root offshoots of an underwater plant, filled with motionless bluish-rose liquid, half corporeal. The lump that is her heart, just below the see-through ribcage, is still and unmoving—yet. As all things form, the translucence also fades, until she is fully opaque.

As she comes back into being, Nairis—or Janerizel—is a life-sized doll, a reposing statue of flesh which is not flesh yet; but wait, now it is.

Once more she is at that interim stage of being where she is already tangible, yet not much more than a hairless smooth thing of poured wax. Beautiful, the Duke again notes and marvels, and feels a distracting surge of warmth—no, stop.

"Now, the final step. . . . Yes!" whispers Molly. "Make her move with life! Make her truly move and be! My Lord, my sweet Duke, I entrust upon your care my sister, Nairis."

And suddenly she clutches Rossian's hand, and through his shirtsleeve he immediately connects to her on a strange level, feels her black flames, a killing destructive force which permeates her, flowing out of the deep maw in her skull. He sees it freely now, death encroaching, at the same time as he remembers the moment of their peculiar oath-bound intimacy, wrist-to-wrist, when yesterday her blood mixes with his.

"What are you doing?" he exclaims, startled out of the

intricacies of the energy manipulation in which he engages over Nairis. Molly's hand continues pressing against his arm, small fingers gripping tight, and involuntarily he feels a strange sympathetic response as something lashes out at her from within him. He feels a grand overpowering wave of strength that seems to ripple out of the fabric of the world; it enters him. It courses up from his genitals, then his solar plexus, and out through his arm and engages hers on an antagonistic occult level.

His life force has been called forth and now it grapples with her unnatural death-energy. Where their flesh touches, even through the shirtsleeves, there is a roiling of temperatures, fire and ice fluctuating at an alarming rate, hot to cold, shuddering, air itself heating and cooling in a rapidfire pulse.

"Molly!" he manages to gasp. "What are you doing? We must not do this—" Yet somehow he is now locked in a feeble state of inaction where he does not find the will in himself to let go of her although he knows he must disengage, while their opposite forces battle. Indeed, there is a buzz of pleasure at the threshold between him and her, a sensual coming together in a mutually canceling-out death wish and life urge.

And yet it seems that the battle is fought on unequal terms. Life force is a moving vector while death is a swallowing maw, and the aggressive overpowers the receptive. Within moments, he is a burning occult torch and he feels his virile life-flames leave his flesh and begin to travel up her arm in a reverse transmutation of energy.

Molly screams, while he knows what is happening to her flesh, how it begins a strange transformation of its own, and yet he is unable to let go, to shake her off, and she is holding on with a desperate grip.

"Promise . . ." she says, as his life force eats up her gaping vacuum, filling her with cleansing destruction. "Promise that you will care for her. Take me . . . take what's left of me and the force, and put me inside her. . . . Put me back inside my Nairis . . . Izelle, oh, my sister, my only love. . . ."

The fey light in her eyes begins to fade together with their entreaty, and suddenly Molly is translucent.

The Duke stares in horror as the strange creature who has insinuated herself into his life only a day ago with an impossible intimacy is fading into nothing, her outlines blurring and her form taking on a remote and infinite distance.

The peacock-bright jester costume collapses into a pile of rags on top of something small and unidentifiable, while in the sudden resulting absence of Molly and Molly's hold, the Duke's arm is released. He falls forward from the recoiling strength of his own resistance, falls hands first against the body of Nairis-Izelle.

Life force is an inferno now, as it consumes the place which is Molly and beyond; consumes the chamber and lashes out for the second time, entering the static body on the bed.

It's as though the heavens have opened up for an instant and divine lightning courses through him. The Duke groans in unexpected sexual release, feeling it blast from the center in his genitals, for suddenly he is hard and erect without trying, and on the next exhalation of breath he comes, groaning in one continuous guttural sound, comes in his clothes, weak-kneed, staining himself, while the energy continues through him, through his hands, and out into the body. . . .

The body jerks with the charge, and she sits up, chest first, head still lolling, hairless and incomplete, as the heart begins a shuddering terrible pounding, running double-time. At the same instant, other organs engage as the intricate mechanism cranks into being—brain, lungs, liver, pancreas, kidneys, spleen, stomach, intestines, womb—and the liquid in her veins is stirred to movement and begins to advance, so that in less then five beats her skin attains color, while hair begins to appear from the follicles.

Another full-body spasm, and Nairis-Izelle opens her eyes wide, and on her first regular breath lets out a scream. It is the raw cracked-voice sound of a Mad Queen, and for the first time in decades, possibly at least a century, it fills the recesses of stone and resounds with familiarity in the Mad Queens Tower.

The newborn woman then sits up, clutching her naked body with her arms, her legs folded at the knees, panting rapidly, staring wildly about her. And yet, when she sees the Duke and says, "Oh, God . . . Oh, God!" over and over, there is clarity and reason in her cornflower-blue eyes, for she is fully herself and cognizant and alive.

"Molly . . ." the Duke says stupidly, half bent, fallen near her on the bed, propping himself with the elbows. There is a spreading stain at his crotch, but neither he nor Izelle-Nairis seem to notice or care, not in this moment post-miracle.

"Molly! Oh, my Molly, where—" and the woman bursts into shuddering sobs. Fat tears run down her face which is now red and imperfect and contorted with genuine pain.

The Duke watches her and cannot help but notice such detail; notices the rich auburn hair that once again falls in a tangle around her, and the pale soft skin, and the hollow elegance of her face, so unlike her sister's. . . .

"Where is she?"

And then she looks down and sees the garish costume on the floor, mere steps away from the bed.

Her face is a mess of anguish. Nairis—or Izelle—makes fists to beat at herself. She grabs the coverlet and the bedding around her and covers herself, shuddering, and again she strikes her chest as she repeats, "In here . . . She is in here."

ಣಧ VII ಶ

Parting Gift

In the early evening, the castle is an exuberantly burning candle, containing in itself a reflection of rose and persimmon and warm peach sunset. The stones of granite seem to acquire color, rich saturated hues of the earth and sky, entwined.

The Duchess of White is departing tonight, for she will not stay to sleep in these walls, not a moment longer than necessary. With her restoration to life, she has lost her powers.

As a result, she now has her freedom.

It is a curious blessing, this gain through loss, the Duke considers, for he is still in a shock, in a haze of spent effort and furious regret and. . . .

Molly.

"It started a very long time ago," the Duchess of White tells him, as she stands before him in his study, primly dressed in borrowed clothing and radiating cold closed-in composure. He realizes she is still wary of him and of the world in general (and will be so for quite a long time), and she longs to be gone, and yet she does him the favor of an explanation.

"A long time ago I was a lonely little girl. I had no sister, you must understand. Molly—she is not real. I made her myself, made her from the budding powers in me that I was just discovering. I had a doll—a favorite toy, or maybe my only toy, after my parents died, leaving me to insane solitude. And so my Molly and I 'played' pretend games. Until one day I gave her enough of my life force that she came alive. She's me, you know—*was* me. I fragmented myself in two, unknowingly, so that I would be with someone, and in the process, I think this was the beginning of the corruption of my powers. A living being is a complete self-sustaining entity of very specific balanced elements joined together in cosmic attraction—must always be so in order to retain true cohesion. Life energy is not to be measured in random portions, not to be doled out in casual bits and droplets like some homogenous stuff poured from a jar of milk. Instead it is a complex energy construct with a precise required proportion of elemental particles that together make a greater whole."

"Yes," he says. "I realize it now."

"When Molly grew sufficiently autonomous (but never truly complete, of course; I was so ignorant of the nature of these things then), with time she became stronger, larger—full human size—and I think I continued to 'feed' her being with the small constant radiation from my own living self in the form of affection, need, love. Molly was a wonder—she was my companion and my confidante and my joy—the best of myself. We made up names and games and we lost ourselves in the interaction. We grew, both of us. I would forget she was unreal, and in time she forgot that she was not a child of my parents.

Though—on some deep level I think she always knew."

"She knew enough, when she came here, with you. . . ." the Duke says, watching her.

"Yes," the Duchess says. "I think she wanted more than anything to be alive, to be her own being. And yet—it was the critical foolhardy time when I had the idea of breaking out of the prison of my castle. We stood at the gates, and she passed across somehow (probably the barrier recognized her occult *incompleteness* as a being and allowed her through). I enacted the ritual, and felt my power—my very self!—drain out of me and into her. I stepped across the barrier, free, I thought. And the next instant, she did as I asked, she poured it all back into me. . . . I only remember a fierce instant of pain, and then nothing. Until today, when you brought me back."

"So you do not remember . . . being alive in the interim, yesterday?"

But the Duchess looks at him blankly, and he does not pursue the line of thought.

"I must thank you with all my heart," Izelle says, and she puts her hand forth.

The Duke takes it in his own and feels absolutely nothing neither a surge of power nor recoil nor emotion. He lifts it to his mouth and there is indifferent, lukewarm softness at his lips.

"What will you do now?" he asks in politeness.

A tiny living smile comes to her lips for the first time. Her lips, the Duke notices, they are wide and full and sensual. Completely different. And somehow it makes him remember a different rosebud mouth.

"What will I do? Why, anything and everything," says the Duchess of White. "I will return to my castle long enough to make arrangements, then travel the world and *live* at last, truly live. So much time to make up, you know, so much fierce joy. And—what of you? I realize that with your considerable arcane ability you now have complete control over the barrier, my Lord. You may simply walk out of these gates and also go wherever you please. It's such a glorious realm we live in, so much beauty to see and experience—"

"Yes," he says. "True, so much beauty out there, indeed." And then he adds, "But, I don't think I will."

She frowns, drawing her smooth brow into a crease. "What? Whyever not?"

And the Duke thinks in that moment how, knowing what he knows now, he can rip at the barrier and pull down the universal drapery, and make the whole of creation dissolve just like Molly. . . . And he thinks that the Duchess, without her powers, and now forever locked away from the tree of knowledge with its impossible terrible fruit, will not understand it even if he tries to explain.

And so he smiles a little, a sad nostalgic movement of his face. And he says, to mollify her, "Maybe, someday."

Mollify her, he thinks, ponders the double meaning of the word. *It is one thing I cannot do.*

"One more matter—I'm in your debt, my Lord," the Duchess says, as she prepares to leave the room. "If there is anything I can do for you—nothing could ever be sufficient or adequate recompense for the magnitude of your act of course, but, anything—please do let me know."

"There is one thing . . ." he says softly, watching the auburn glorious flow of her hair as she turns from him. And then, half-turned, she pauses. There is a long instant of tangible silence between them, and just possibly, she understands.

"Oh, I think I know," she says then; indeed, she does. She reaches to open the infamous box of remains that is concealed by the width of her skirts, and which she takes with her like a lady's purse.

The lock clicks, and inside, on a bed of velvet, is a child's toy. An old porcelain doll with matted well-loved hair, a tussled old wig, her stuffed fabric body dressed in bright peacock hand-sewn finery of an archaic jester. Her head is pale and appears to have a rosy-soft veneer even though he knows just underneath it is a hard shell of smooth porcelain, and her glass eyes are dark and huge and somewhat weird, surrounded by a real fringe of eyelashes and skillfully-made lids that open and close.

She has a tiny button nose and a rosebud mouth.

At the sight of her, the Duke's chest—something deep inside there, a complex machinery—painfully constricts.

"Thank you," he says, reaching for the doll.

He stands, holding Molly with one stiff hand against his own chest, while the Duchess of White exits the room, and then, he knows, forever leaves his castle.

She will not return. And who could blame her?

There is freedom, out there. But not for him.

The greatest living master of the arcane, the magus of the highest order, the man who can bring the dead to life, stands still, watching the sun set from the familiar hated-and-beloved window of his study.

Later yet, as the night sets in and the stars come out to fill heaven with firefly light, the Duke climbs the wind-funnel stairwell of the Mad Queens Tower and walks up on the roof. He leans between the tall, thick merlons, watching the well of sky overhead—it is almost a full dome, but not quite.

The doll is still clutched against his chest. And once again he believes he hears inside him the heavy tedious sound of ever-slowing clockwork.

He looks out, over into the blind darkness of distance, the unseen expanse that is the whole world—it is at his mercy, subject to his stewardship and ultimate responsibility. And yet, power is in his mind now, a vortex of death and life. He feels, without needing to see, the wind of the world on his face, the distant waters and the firmament held at bay, and imagines the sand road, below, occluded in darkness.

All of it, everything, is permeated with the life force. It is a world of crystalline nodes with infinite facets.

Rossian, the Duke of Violet stands perfectly still and opens his mind, and lets the life force that he now rules so well enter and course through him, no longer resisting its truth. It is infinitely easy then, how the Duke takes a step in his mind and flies, moving along the everlasting plateau of nodes, without ever leaving his castle.

ೞ೦ಔ THE END ೲೲಜಿ

Author's Note

I started writing this one in the mid-80s, when in college, and could neither properly finish nor set it aside. Over the years the ideas and characters and storyline haunted me, mutated and grew in complexity, and the compounding of meanings became more layered than an onion.

    As with any obsession, you must first understand it before you can let go.

    I think I finally can.

Vera Nazarian
Los Angeles, CA
February 21, 2008

Acknowledgements

My heart and my thanks to the many friends who helped me immensely with this work—Paul Barnett, Giles Bignold, Stella Bloom, David Bloom, Anne Bussell, Michael Ehart, Catherine Mintz, Anna Tambour, Brook West, Paul Witcover, and last but not least, the Spinners who were Jim Brunet, Megan Christopher, Steve Ford, Susan Franzblau, Gary Glass, Harry Ingham, Davy Krieger, and Jenn Reese.

www.ingramcontent.com/pod-product-compliance
Lightning Source LLC
Chambersburg PA
CBHW030145200626
46812CB00015B/1699